Dawn sat unmoving as Brian placed his hands on her throat and brushed his way around to the outline of her collarbone. Inside she was being ignited into a thousand flames, but somehow she willed herself to remain still. This moment was one she'd given up dreaming would ever happen. Although it took the utmost in self-control, Dawn was determined to experience it to the fullest.

A soft sigh escaped her lips as Brian's exploring fingers found the soft swell of her breasts. He met her mouth with lips that knew how to trigger the fullest emotion of a woman. The inner flame expanded, coursing through her limbs until she wondered if she was on the verge of passing out. Ecstasy was the goal her body craved...demanded!

ABOUT THE AUTHOR

Vella Munn's love for baseball stems from her sons' involvement in the sport. She has served as a player agent and scorekeeper for a farm team of the Oakland A's club. Vella resides in Oregon and this is her first published romance novel.

Summer Season

VELLA MUNN

Harlequin Books

TORONTO • NEW YORK • LONDON
AMSTERDAM • PARIS • SYDNEY • HAMBURG
STOCKHOLM • ATHENS • TOKYO • MILAN

Published February 1984

First printing December 1983

ISBN 0-373-16042-9

Printed in Canada

Chapter One

For several moments Dawn Morrell stood poised on the topmost steps overlooking Verdue Field. The breeze toyed with her long white-blond hair, kissed cheekbones deeply toasted through a lifelong love affair with the sun, and lifted her spirits in a way that was both ageless and newborn.

"I'm home," she whispered into the silent space that reached out to the four-hundred-foot center-field fence. "Oh, yes, I'm home."

The wind answered with a message of its own, unwrapping the American flag from around the white pole and sending it streaming to the west as night settled over the field. Dawn had stood in awe before a thousand flags in her twenty-seven years, but her response to the symbol of her country never changed. A lump born of pride rose in her throat and brought tears to her sapphire eyes. This was where she belonged. She'd finally made peace with her restless spirit. As surely as she knew she could never stem that spirit within the white corridors of Cook County Hospital, she bowed in acceptance before the knowledge that she wasn't made for walls and doors, union meetings, and schedules tacked to bulletin boards. The Rogue Valley meant clear skies, virgin air, the surrounding forest. It wasn't perfect. There was an unresolved past to come to grips with—a man and one magic night—but at least she could stretch out her arms and feel the freedom here.

Slowly, because this early spring night belonged to her and her need to take stock of herself, she made her way down the wooden stairs. The grass at Verdue Field lay rich and thick, ready for cleats, sliding bodies, hard hit ground balls. Whoever had been in charge of the grounds since she left the Rogue Valley to go to college was someone of considerable skill. Dawn had played enough softball and attended enough baseball games to know that the healthy green carpet didn't remain that way without constant care. The infield diamond had been painstakingly turned and tamped and finished with a fine red layer of crushed rock. It provided a vivid contrast to the rich green that stretched to the outfield fences. The base paths and batter's box hadn't been chalked but since the season wasn't due to begin for several more weeks, there was no need.

Dawn reached the ground, her canvas running shoes landing silently on the cement walkway. She stepped forward and wrapped her fingers through the Cyclone fencing that protected fans from careening foul balls. For a moment she pressed her face against the man-made barrier, seeing not the approaching night but what would always remain in her memory. As a child she'd watched many games from such a position, ignoring her mother's warning about the risk of injury to face and fingers. In those days her father played on one of the local fast pitch softball teams, and Dawn's happiest moments were spent watching him on the mound, throwing one low fastball after another past frustrated batters.

"You did it to me, Dad," she told the ghosts of a thousand ballplayers who had run the bases or stood ready in the outfield in the thirty-year history of Verdue Field. "You're the one who got me hooked on baseball. And the outdoor life. The country hick has come home."

Dad would be proud of her. Even as she fought off the quiet sorrow that had been part of her since his death, she sensed that he was still here in some way, nodding his gray head because he knew what it was like to have baseball and a spring breeze in one's blood. There was no fighting it. Verdue Field was where Dawn Morrell belonged.

Maybe it was the old baseball jersey she was wearing. Maybe it was the multiwashed faded sweat pants hanging from her hips. Whatever the reason, Dawn knew her visit to Verdue Field wouldn't be complete until she'd run the bases. She'd done just that a hundred times during her teenage years, when she played for the Thunderbird softball team, but not here, not at one of the finest baseball complexes in the Northwest. She'd had to play on fields maintained by the parks and recreation department, while Verdue Field remained reserved for the American Legion and the two semipro teams in the valley.

But Dawn was now officially part of the professional A's farm team organization. She had as much right to this diamond as any of the rookie team members who would soon arrive to play in the Northwest

League. She'd be out there working with them every day. Why shouldn't she give in to the child still living within the adult? Besides, it was nearly dark. Who could see her? she thought.

She walked over to the home team's dugout and up the two steps that led to the playing field itself. For a moment she was all kid again, timid, hoping no one would see her, waiting for someone to chase her off. But only silence, broken by the ever-present wind, reached her ears. Tonight she was alone, free to do whatever she wanted.

Skipping a little from excitement, she made her way first to the on deck circle swinging an imaginary bat in slow, muscle-relaxing circles. She squinted slightly, eyes on the phantom batter poised at home plate. "Wait for your pitch," she called out to the teammate who existed only in her mind. "You like them low and inside."

Yes, there it was! The pitcher was young and strong, but he hadn't done his homework. The fast-ball was low and inside, just what her teammate had been waiting for. The ball connected solidly with the bat, the ageless sound of wood finding its mark. Dawn's eyes never left the line drive that shot through the hole between third and short.

A two-bagger!

Now the pressure was on her. There was a runner in scoring position. A solid single, and she'd have an RBI to her credit. Dawn turned toward the coach standing near third base, nodding slightly to let him know she'd read his signal. Swing away. Go for the fence. Ah, yes, that's what she wanted. No sacrifice bunt for Dawn Morrell. After all, wasn't she the team's cleanup hitter? They relied on her to produce.

And produce was what she was determined to do. Slowly, confident, eyes on the now flustered pitcher, she took her position in the batter's box, swinging the trusty bat that had been her constant companion all year. Dawn took a second to glance back at the crouching catcher. He was busy flashing signs to the pitcher, but Dawn was used to that. It didn't matter what they decided on—curve, slider, fastball. Dawn Morrell could hit everything they threw at her.

She waited. The first ball was outside the strike zone. Good! The pitcher was afraid to throw her a fat pitch. She let the second ball—a strike—go by. She could be patient, wait for the one she wanted.

There it was, waist high and slightly outside. Dawn swung with a level, fluid motion, twisting her wrists at the exact split second it took to give her that extra ounce of strength.

Crack!

She was off and digging hard, driving toward first, eyes both on the high and handsome arc of the ball and the base. She could feel it in her chest, in the very air she breathed. Like Reggie Jackson, she delighted in watching her home runs reach their mark. As she neared first she slowed. There was no reason to hurry now—that ball was out of there!

Dawn trotted easily around the bases, acknowledging the cheers from the crowd, the yells of encouragement from her teammates. Home run! And in Verdue Field too! That would make the front page of the local paper all right.

She was breathing easily as she neared home and jumped squarely on the rubber with both feet. Put that one in the record books. Four-hundred-foot shot, at least.

"Hey, you missed second!"

Dawn jumped, her heart pounding wildly. The voice, totally unexpected in the empty diamond, was like a bucket of cold water in her face. As she turned, trying to trace the source of the voice, she blushed beet red under her tan. Someone had seen her game. Whoever he was, he'd watched her swing her make-believe bat and raise her arms in a victory sign when the nonexistent ball sailed over the center field fence.

Finally, she spotted him standing half hidden in the deep shadows of the dugout along the first base side. If her life depended on it, Dawn couldn't have moved. Instead, she stood on home plate, wishing with everything she had for a shovel so she could dig a hole to climb into.

Twenty-seven-year-old women don't hit phantom balls and run the bases on a baseball field that has just been leased by a major league baseball club for one of its farm teams, she thought. Someday she might be able to laugh at this. Tonight, however, was not one of those times.

The man spoke again. "I said, you missed second. Ump, she missed second. The batter is out!"

Something about the voice tugged at Dawn's memory. It had a place in her teenage years, didn't it? she wondered. If only he'd come out of the shadows, she would know who had invaded her solitude. But then she'd have to admit she'd just made a complete fool of herself. "I did not miss second," she shot back, astonished that she had any voice at all.

The man made his way out of the dugout and stood

on the green carpet that was the foul area for the first base side of the diamond. He was tall; she could tell that his hair was as dark as hers was light. Once again her memory stirred, but in her confusion and embarrassment she was unable to concentrate on anything except the ridiculous position she was in. "I said you missed the bag," he insisted. "I ought to know. I was watching the whole thing. Tell you what. You go back to second, and we won't say anything more about it."

"What are you doing here? No one's supposed to be here." Dawn had recovered enough to be gathering her wits about her. The man appeared to have a sense of humor, and that helped. It was embarrassing—terribly embarrassing—but it wasn't the first thing she'd done in her life to bring a flush of color to her cheeks. It probably wouldn't be the last.

"I climbed over the fence," the man said as he came closer. "You know how it is when you don't have the price of admission. You have to be innovative. You won't call the cops or anything, will you?"

He was only a few feet away, but it was too dark to make out his features. Dawn didn't try to think of a response to his bit of nonsense. The stirring in her mind was stronger than ever. Who was he? she asked herself. Somewhere, somehow, their paths had crossed. "I know you, don't I? Your voice sounds familiar."

"Funny,' he said. "I was thinking the same thing. There aren't that many women with hair that's almost white. And that tan. I've seen that before. You look like you should have a surfboard under your arm, not a baseball mitt."

"I'm hardly a surfer," Dawn supplied. "In fact,

I've never been in the ocean in my life. I'm a nurse."

He shook his head. "You're no nurse. Where's your white uniform and white stockings? Or don't nurses wear those things anymore?"

Dawn laughed. She'd been seen doing the most ridiculous thing a former emergency room nurse could be accused of. Why not make the most of it? she thought. She hadn't broken any laws, and at twenty-seven she was no longer so dependent on the opinions of others. "I can't hit home runs in white stockings. I traded them in on a batting helmet."

"You still missed second." The man stuck out a broad hand. "I'm Brian Riegel. What's your name? Lefty? You were switch-hitting out there."

Brian Riegel! A moonlit party with music, wine, college boys, and a young, inexperienced high-school girl! "You? I don't believe it!" she stammered. The events of a few minutes ago hadn't struck her dumb, but this had. Of all the people to meet during her first visit to Verdue Field in nine years, why was it Brian Riegel? she wondered.

"So my name rings a bell, does it? I knew we knew each other. Aren't you going to tell me yours?"

Would it mean anything to him? she asked herself. It was so long ago, and it was only one night. At least for him it was one night. It had lasted much, much longer for her. "I'm Dawn Morrell," she whispered. "I grew up in the valley, same as you. I guess you could say we revolved in different circles."

"You went to the local high school. My God, it really is you. What happened to you after you graduated? You went east to go to college, didn't you? Didn't your dad die last year?"

He knew that much about her. The realization shook her. Just because she'd been sucked in by the magic of the one evening they'd shared didn't mean he'd felt the same. Of course he hadn't. He'd never asked her out. "Did you know my father?" Dawn asked, suddenly anxious to turn her thoughts away from that night.

"Not really. Oh, I knew he was a lawyer. This valley is small enough that most of the lawyers get their names in the paper from time to time. He wasn't involved in criminal law, was he? I thought about becoming a lawyer once, but that's as far as it went."

"My father's firm specialized in business contracts, setting up corporations, that sort of thing. But weren't you going to college to become an architect?"

"At the beginning. I changed my major three times in those four years, much to my parents' consternation. I'm sure they breathed a sigh of relief when my business venture in Washington proved a success." Brian ran his hand through his black hair as if irritated with himself. "You were in high school. I was going to the local college. That's right, isn't it?"

"We also went to high school together," Dawn supplied. "But I was an underclassman, while you were an exalted senior. I'm sure you didn't know I was alive back then."

"Don't be so sure, Dawn. I might have been filled with my own self-importance, but I wasn't blind. You had to be the only girl in school with white hair."

"I'm not sure about that. But I probably was the only one whose hair color didn't come out of a bottle." She laughed and then relented, thinking back to the first time she became aware of Brian Riegel in her life. Ten years had passed since that last meeting. Surely in that time he'd lost the hold he once had on her, she thought. "I went to a football game. You were the wide receiver. That's the first time I noticed you."

One moment Dawn was looking up into Brian's deep brown eyes, and the next, he had folded his long legs under him and was sitting cross-legged on the grass. He patted the ground next to him. "I've been on my feet all day. How about if we get comfortable? Those were the days," he said softly, almost sadly, as she joined him. "Talk about the exalted senior. I thought there was no stopping me then. After all, I was on the varsity football team. I had an ego that wouldn't quit, I'm afraid. I had my future all mapped out. Four years of college on a sports scholarship, and then sit back and wait for the pro offers to come in." A light left his nut-brown eyes. "That's before my knees went out on me. The pros don't want a sticky-fingered wide receiver with surgery scars on his knees. That's what brought me to the business world."

"I'm sorry." Despite the night, Dawn could see it in his eyes. The dream had died hard. "Do you enjoy what you're doing now?"

He took her hand, ran his fingers along the smooth skin for a moment, and then let go. "I've made a certain peace with myself. It's made me cynical and wary, but I don't suppose it can be helped. At least things are looking up from a few months ago."

Dawn didn't respond. The light touch had left her momentarily speechless. Her flesh had come alive the way it did when wind and sunlight kissed it. Did he have any idea what he'd done to her during that brief contact? she wondered. "What do you mean?" she asked. "What were you doing?"

"Nothing of any account. Making a living." His eyes found hers in the growing dusk and let her inside him, telling her that the time of joking had, for the moment, passed. There were tiny lines around his eyes that hadn't been there when they were growing up, but the years had added character to his face. He'd been handsome when she fell under his spell, but in those days his eyes hadn't said much about the man behind the exterior. Now he was a man who hadn't shaved since morning, whose hair had surrendered to the wind's strength, whose flesh admitted its hours under a drying sun. His shoulders were still broad, his waist tapered, but no longer did he carry himself with a self-possessed air. Something had happened to Brian Riegel over the years to make him comfortable or at least at peace with who he was. She imagined he no longer cared whether his clothes were of the latest style or whether he was the center of attention.

"I heard you moved to Washington after you finished college," Dawn said when she realized they'd been silent for several moments. "What brought you back here?"

"I don't like rain. I was starting to mold." He smiled again and because they were sitting so close, she could see the lines tugging at the corners of his mouth. "No. That isn't the whole story. I'd reached burnout in more ways than one. I found out I wasn't suited for the gray-flannel-suit life. I wanted something else. I found it here—at least part of it."

"Me too," Dawn said.

"Are you serious?"

"I'll tell you the long, complicated story later," she countered. He'd touched her curiosity with his comment about what he was doing with his life now. She wasn't about to let him change the subject. "You were working and living in Washington. You said something about having your own business. But now you're here. What happened?"

"Do you have time for the complete saga?" He glanced at his watch. "Look, I haven't eaten yet. Do you have to go anywhere?"

Dawn still hadn't unpacked all of her boxes after moving into the little house she had bought just outside the city limits, but because she hadn't made any friends yet, the prospect of spending the night alone made her feel restless. Besides, she'd much rather be with Brian. "I was going to feed my face. After all, hitting home runs burns up the calories."

He helped her to her feet and then steered her toward the exit, his arm casually around her shoulders. "How about pizza? You know it's traditional during baseball season."

"Can we get away with that? The season hasn't started yet." Maybe she shouldn't be so casual about letting him put his arm around her, she thought, but they weren't strangers. They'd known each other since the time when a hero-worshipping high school student developed a crush on a big football star. Besides, his arm felt warm and protective. It was a feeling she'd been denied lately.

"It has for me. Do you remember Knight's? I just rediscovered it. The owners finally learned how to make pizza, or maybe it's under new ownership. Anyway, their sourdough crust can't be beat. Are you willing to take a chance on it?"

Dawn threw back her head as the night-cooled breeze caught her hair. "You are talking to one of the world's great pizza lovers. I've made a study of such establishments my hobby."

"You don't look like it." His eyes slid down her frame and came back to rest on her slim shoulders.

"Fortunately, I'm one of those who has the metabolism to go with my appetite," she responded quickly to hide a small shiver set off by the effect of his eyes on her. "I'm also a fanatic about exercise. Otherwise I'd have to wear tents instead of jeans."

The only other vehicle outside Verdue Field besides Dawn's white compact was a large new van bearing the words *A's Baseball—Verdue Field*, painted in black on the pale green surface. Brian grabbed the handle and opened the passenger side. "This is yours?" she asked. "I thought it went with the field. That's why I thought no one was here."

"It does. I go with the field. I have my own car, one that fortunately gets much better gas mileage, but because I never know when I'm going to need the stuff I've got crammed into the van, I usually wind up driving it."

The pieces of the puzzle surrounding Brian Riegel were falling into place, but Dawn didn't ask any questions as he started the van and joined the southbound traffic. Brian had something to do with Verdue Field and the newly acquired A's franchise. Did he know the role she was going to be playing in it? Was that why he was saying so little? He could be waiting for her to tip her hand, so to speak, blurt out more than maybe she should about her new job and her impression of the organization.

Well, it wasn't going to happen. Dawn had been a working woman long enough to have learned the value of keeping her own council. Let Brian be the first to speak, she decided.

His first words had nothing to do with baseball. "Awhile ago you said something about having come back home. Don't answer this if you don't want to, but did you get divorced or something and move back here?"

His question was more personal than she'd expected, but she didn't attempt to dodge it. "No. I've never been married. I came back for two reasons. I love this valley, and I wanted to be closer to my mother now that she's alone."

"Career woman. No time for a family?"

"You make it sound like a crime." She bristled, no longer sure that going out to eat with Brian was such a good idea. "Yes, I'm a career woman. At least I guess that's what you call it. I'm a nurse by profession, although I've just changed direction. And I didn't get married because—well, it never happened." Dawn stopped, pulled back into the strange turns her life had taken since high school. She'd always assumed she would be getting married someday and having the children she knew she'd love and nurture, but the man she wanted to father those children simply hadn't entered her life.

Maybe she was asking too much from a man. When she had first laid eyes on Brian Riegel and given her young heart to a dark-haired athlete in shoulder pads, she'd been willing to swear that love was tears in a pillow, a heart that threatened to burst simply because he'd passed her in the hall, music in her head, and stars in her eyes. In the years since then she'd learned otherwise. Men weren't unattainable creatures set up on pedestals. They were breath and soul humans who got speeding tickets, ate with their elbows on the table, and sometimes fell asleep during movies. Dawn no longer held out for the reincarnation of her adolescent fantasies.

But neither had she found a man who could satisfy that strange restless searching in her heart.

Brian broke the silence. "I had no business saying what I did. I'm afraid I've let my personal prejudices enter into the conversation. It's not fair to you."

Dawn nodded. Brian had given her a brief glimpse into himself. She wanted the opportunity to think over his words, but now was not the time. "Wasn't there once a car dealership over there?" she asked as she pointed at a new apartment complex. "I came back for Dad's funeral last year, but I didn't take time to look around. It's changed since I was in high school," she finished.

"I know." Brian signaled and pulled off into the Knight's Pizza parking lot. "I've had the same feelings. I remember things being bigger than they are. I guess that's because I was smaller then and had less control over my life."

"You looked pretty big to me," Dawn observed as they entered the pizza parlor. "When I saw you suited up for a game, I thought you were the biggest player out there."

"You must have missed the defensive linemen. I have those apes to thank for what happened to my knees. Do you like olives?"

Dawn looked at the menu Brian held in his hand. They were standing in front of the counter, surrounded by children, young couples, and teenagers. But for a moment Dawn would have sworn they were the only two people in the dimly lit room. She could feel the warmth of Brian's body through her baseball shirt, a warmth that spread quickly through her and left her legs strangely weak. Did he still have a hold on her after all these years? she wondered once more. She'd been a child then, a naive and untested newcomer to the world of man-woman relationships. Her heart had been so vulnerable, so believing in fairy tales. Did part of her still remain true to that long-ago fantasy that saw the football hero take his princess into his arms and block out the world?

No. That was years ago. Before college. Before working for a living. Before a freak motorcycle accident that changed the course of her life.

Dawn pulled back. Brian Riegel was no longer the campus jock and she a daydreaming teenager. He had scars on his knees. She had lived through a badly broken leg held immobile for months. That was reality, not the lingering memory of one night he had probably forgotten.

After they settled on a sausage pizza, Brian ordered white wine for Dawn and a beer for himself. He steered her into a corner, away from the distraction of video games. "I'm getting older," he offered. "Either that or those machines make more noise than they used to

"Let's not talk about age." Dawn laughed, wrinkling up her nose. "If you promise not to mention how many years it's been since we last saw each other, I won't either."

Brian leaned forward. "The years have been good to you. You said something about being a fanatic about exercise. You weren't kidding, were you?"

Dawn flushed under the casual compliment. "My father was always competing in sports. I guess he laid the groundwork. I didn't get enough exercise when I was working in the hospital, but— Oh, you don't want to hear about that. The less said about a country hick trying to survive in Chicago the better." Dawn shook her head. Leaving the confines of the hospital was the best move she'd made in years. It was also the last thing she wanted to talk about tonight. "Weren't you going to tell me what brought you back here? I have no idea why you're driving the Verdue Field van."

Brian took a sip of his beer, leaned back in his chair, and slowly clasped his hands behind his head, his eyes gleaming in the muted light. "I thought you'd never ask. I don't know if you're aware of this, but the A's have just expanded their baseball franchise. They're adding a farm team to the Northwest League. A farm team is the first rung on the ladder to fame and fortune for a few gifted athletes. You happen to be looking at the new general manager."

There! It had all fallen into place. "Then, you're my boss," Dawn supplied.

Chapter Two

How long had Brian been staring at her? Dawn wondered. She was vaguely aware of sounds and movement around her, hanging plants near the window, the tantalizing scent of spices and cheese, but those were only distant impressions lingering at the corners of her consciousness. Only Brian's eyes and the sudden tension in his forearms were real.

"I'm your boss?" he said at length.

Dawn nodded. Why was he looking at her in that new way as if she were no longer a pleasant acquaintance but rather a strange creature he was holding up for inspection? she asked herself. "Maybe that's not the right way to put it," she offered, desperate to hide her confusion from him. "I was hired by the A's organization. But if you're the general manager, then perhaps I'll be reporting to you."

"In what capacity?" The question was quick and direct. "I don't need a secretary. Besides, didn't you say you were a nurse? The team doesn't need a nurse."

"I'm aware of that," she answered shortly to match his own brusque speech. "But baseball teams have trainers, don't they? My contract says I'm a trainer, so it must be true."

"The organization hired a woman trainer?" The tension was still in Brian's arms and in the fierce way his eyes clung to hers. "The ballplayers won't stand for a female trainer."

"I wish someone had told me that before," Dawn countered. "Why do you think I was allowed to take the National Athletic Trainers Association test? If I'd known that, I certainly wouldn't have worked for eighteen hundred hours under the supervision of a certified athletic trainer."

"What do you know about baseball?"

"Enough. Let's see. At halftime the team at bat gets to go out into the field. Isn't that how it goes?" Was this conversation really happening? she wondered. Most of the men she knew no longer questioned a woman's right to compete in the world on a par with men. Surely Brian Riegel wasn't a throwback to the dark ages. "I'm not going to pretend I could take over managing a team, but I do know what it takes to keep an athlete in top physical shape, including proper diet, and how to come back from an injury. That's what I've been hired to accomplish."

"Nothing to it?" Brian asked. "Is that what you're saying?"

She stopped him. "I won't admit it was easy convincing the franchise's owners that I could handle the job, but I know anatomy and nutrition. I also know that the brain and the body have to work together. They bought that." She allowed herself a smile. "Of course, a few letters of recommendation from my instructors at Cal Poly didn't hurt. I had to go back to college to pick up some courses in injury prevention, the physiology of exercise, that sort of thing, while I was getting in my lab hours. They spoke highly of me."

"I'm listening," he challenged.

If Dawn hadn't been so enthusiastic about her change in career direction since her motorcycle accident, she might have faltered under Brian's words, but if there was one aspect of her life she felt comfortable with, this was it. She met his eyes straight on as she told him about the years of study it had taken to become a nurse, the first enthusiastic months when she dressed in a white uniform and passed out pills and nodded agreeably at doctors' orders. Slowly, however, the newness wore off. Dawn managed to get herself assigned to the emergency room at Cook County Hospital because she was a woman who thrived on challenge and pressure. But night after night of watching people being patched back together—holding the hand of a terrified child, hot tears on her shoulder from the widow of a heart attack victim—was doing things to her she didn't like. Dawn was slowly closing herself off from the suffering of others. She realized her reaction for the defense mechanism it was: "Laugh so you won't cry." But Dawn had become a nurse because she had feelings for people. The change wasn't something she could live with.

"I was restless, dissatisfied. I felt as if I were walking a tightrope between feeling too much and not feeling enough. It got to the point where I knew I had to make a radical change," she told the silent Brian. "But I had to support myself, and I couldn't turn my back on all those years of education. That's when Jim and I had our motorcycle accident."

"Jim?"

"A man I was dating," she explained simply. "Jim was a charter pilot. He also did parachuting. He—Jim was was born in high gear. The only time he ever slowed down was when he was injured."

"I thought you were going to tell me about how you came to be a trainer for a baseball team," Brian interrupted. "I don't need to hear all about your boyfriend."

"He's part of it," she pressed, determined not to be sidetracked. No. Brian was no longer a young girl's daydream. He was a flesh and blood man—irritating and opinionated. "I broke my left leg. *Shattered* is a more accurate description. I spent a month in the hospital. Jim was nearly killed."

Dawn dropped her eyes. No matter how many times she'd gone over those terrifying moments when the motorcycle they were riding just after dawn one Sunday morning went out of control on a haphazardly patched stretch of highway, she'd never been able to stop the cold rush of fear. She still remembered the pain, the lonely darkness on the deserted highway before help came. Somehow she'd been able to drag herself, shattered leg and all, over to where Jim lay unconscious and cradle his limp head in her lap. She hadn't known then that it would be two weeks before he would wake up—and six months before they knew he would walk again.

"His back was broken," Dawn explained. "The doctors didn't know how badly his spinal cord was damaged. Jim went through a year of physical therapy before he could walk without a cane. It nearly destroyed him not to be able to function the way he used to. He was depressed. It was a very dark period for him. I stayed with him the whole time."

Brian took her cold fingers in his own warm hands and lifted them to his lips, breathing life back into them. "He's all right now?"

"I think so. He'll never be able to do some of the things he used to take for granted. The doctors say that's what is delaying him in taking control of his life again." Brian's unexpected gesture gave Dawn the incentive to voice her concerns about Jim. "I'm afraid I tried to protect him too much. I dealt with the insurance company, paid his bills, even convinced his boss to rehire him. Now I see that I wasn't really helping him. I turned into a mother substitute when he should have stood on his own two feet. I'm convinced he'll be better off without me. I—I haven't said that to anyone, especially not to Jim. I don't know why I'm talking about it now." But maybe she did. Maybe it had to do with the man holding her hands.

"Where is he now?"

"He's still in Chicago."

"And you're here. Doesn't that put a strain on your relationship?" Brian's hands were still gentle, but there was nothing relenting about the message in his eyes.

"That's a long story," Dawn countered. "One I'm sure you're no more interested in hearing than I am in telling. Besides, I thought I was supposed to be telling you about how the accident led up to what I'm doing now, not the saga of an overprotective nurse."

"That's right. Forgive me." Brian dropped his head in an exaggerated apology. "Are we into chapter two yet?"

What was he doing to her? One moment she had the feeling Brian was interested in her, and the next he had her convinced he was simply being polite. Through it all was the unsettling feeling that he was putting a barrier between them that wouldn't let emotions through. Maybe if he'd let go of her hands, she could think clearer. But she wasn't sure she wanted to lose the sensation of being placed in his care. "I told you I spent a great deal of time with Jim when he was in physical therapy. For a while I thought I might turn to that field. But Jim was one of the lucky ones. Too many of those there will never get out of their wheelchairs."

"And that depressed you. You didn't like facing stark reality."

Dawn tried to jerk her hands away, but Brian held on. "No, you don't," he warned. "I'm not going to let you off the hook that easily. Dawn, whether either of us likes it, it looks as if we're going to be working together. You may find my methods distasteful at times, but I want to know what kind of woman I'm going to be dealing with. Even a purely professional relationship involves the interacting of personalities. I want you to be honest with me. You don't like being around those hopeless cases, do you?"

"Do you blame me? I told you emergency room work was hardening me to the feelings of others. I didn't want it to continue." It was so easy for him to throw her weakness at her. He wasn't the one who'd talked with a teenage boy who would never walk again, who'd listened to a woman whose dreams of a normal life had been shattered. "Some people are able to work with hopeless cases. I have the greatest admiration in the world for them. I turned in another direction."

"What?"

"I've always enjoyed sports, being active. It was through physical therapy that I became aware of the field of sports medicine." Dawn took a breath and then hurried on. She was excited about what she'd been doing since the cast came off her leg. It didn't matter what Brian might think of her enthusiasm. As long as he was here he was going to have to listen to it. "Not all the people in physical therapy were as badly injured as Jim. I met a lot of people who had been injured through participation in one sport or another and were at the hospital to rebuild strength in muscles, tendons, ligaments. That's when I started to see that many of those injuries didn't have to happen if people knew more about how their bodies worked. Exercise and training is the key. That's what I kept hearing from the staff. My research reinforced that."

"Is that the end of the lecture?" Brian relinquished her hands as their pizza was delivered. He separated a piece for each of them and bit into his own before continuing. "So what you've been doing is in the area of sports medicine. You must have really impressed the organization for them to have hired you."

"It looks that way, doesn't it," she said, facing the challenge in his words. "In case you're not aware of it, there's more to winning games than parking a ball over the center field fence. That ball isn't going to get out of the infield unless the man swinging the bat has developed his muscles to their maximum efficiency. The man has to have an understanding of the machine that's his body. Sports medicine isn't just putting on bandages, Mr. Riegel. It's learning how to prevent injuries through conditioning. That's what I intend to do for the young men who will be playing at Verdue Field. And that's exactly what I told the men who interviewed me.''

"That's a noble pursuit. Your pizza is getting cold.''

"Quite true. And a cold pizza to the true fan is like a foul tip when you're swinging for the fence. Eating has priority right now." Dawn ate in silence. She was uncomfortably aware of Brian's eyes on her even as she concentrated on keeping melted cheese on the crust. Was he really that critical of her ability to work with the young men who'd signed contracts with a professional baseball franchise? she thought. He'd been easygoing enough at Verdue Field. But something, some wall, had been thrown up since then. She knew what a general manager's responsibilities were—dealing with the business end of running a team rather than managing or coaching. In that case he was probably only minimally concerned with such things as practice schedules and training techniques. Why, then, the criticism?

"I've been thinking," Brian said as he selected his second piece. "This might work out to my advantage.''

"Your advantage? I don't understand.''

"You probably don't. I was hired to make this farm team a successful business venture. One of my major concerns is filling the stands. If I let it out through the media that the team has a female trainer—a young, attractive female trainer... You can see the possibilities, can't you?''

"Yes, I can. Unfortunately."

Brian chuckled. "I do believe the lady in question feels I'm taking advantage of her. You don't like having anything to do with the business end of this venture of ours, do you."

"No, I don't. I was hired to help prepare the players for a season of playing ball, not making money for some cigar-smoking owners I'll probably never meet."

"If someone wasn't concerned with money, you wouldn't have a job for long. I'm afraid you can't deny that."

She relented. "You're right. I can't. I just don't like the idea of you exploiting me." Dawn paused long enough to make sure he was looking at her before she continued, "Brian, we go back a long way. Or doesn't that come into consideration?"

A frown creased Brian's forehead. "I guess it's time one of us brought that up, isn't it? That was years ago, Dawn. I'm afraid I don't have much use for the past. It's the present that concerns me."

"I understand," she said softly, wondering if she really did understand. "Are you trying to tell me you want us to act as if we never knew each other?"

"Hardly. That would serve no purpose. What I'm saying is that we've changed since then. We're no longer a couple of kids with no idea of what the world is really about. I know I hadn't had any cold doses of reality. I have now. Whatever relationship we might have had is just that—finished business."

He didn't want to go back. But why should he? There'd only been that one night when the local college football team threw a celebrating party and Dawn had attended with one of her girl friends. She'd hoped—prayed—Brian Riegel would notice her. But even in her wildest dreams she'd never imagined the night would be so perfect. And now he was saying there was no purpose in reopening that chapter in their lives.

"I just wish I hadn't been so impressionable," she said, striving for a light tone. "There were a million girls with their eyes on you. I'd just entered the dating game. I'm sure the evening had much more of an impact on me than it did on you."

"Don't be so sure." He leaned toward her and brushed her hair away from her eyes. "It was my freshman year. My knee hadn't given out on me yet, but that was just around the corner. I'm afraid that bit of reality takes precedence over other things that happened that year. Wasn't there some kind of party?"

"I believe that's what they called it." Dawn was stalling. Of course she remembered. Every detail of that night was embedded in her memory, her heart. How could she forget any of it?

Brian nodded. "Some of the members of the football team were renting a big old house. There were five or six of us living there. I don't think the landlord had any idea what he was in for. We held the party in the backyard. Someone had invited some of the high-school girls. You came."

"I came." Oh, yes, she had come full of dreams and fears, terrified that Brian Riegel would never notice the girl who'd almost died when he had graduated from high school. She'd been able to hold on only because he was going to college locally. She could drive over to the college football field every Saturday night and watch him perform before thousands of screaming fans.

"We spent the evening together."

Dawn jumped, senses brought back to life as completely as they'd been that night years ago. She knew he was waiting for her to nod, to say something, but she couldn't. He remembered. No matter what passed between them in the days and weeks to come, he now knew the details of that night. It was certain to color their relationship from now on.

"That was a long time ago, Brian," she managed, whispering because the past's hold on her was too strong for anything else. "We never saw each other again."

"I know. I transferred to another college after I realized my playing days were over."

And I came close to dying inside. "I—I was so young then," she stammered. "I'm not the same person at all anymore."

"The years change us all." Brian was no longer looking at her. Instead his eyes had strayed to a group of small children huddled around a pinball machine with an Out Of Order sign taped to it. The youngest child, not yet of school age, was standing on tiptoe but still not tall enough to see the top. "I wonder if that little boy will remember what it felt like to be too small to keep up with the older kids," he said softly. "It isn't easy being a child. They have the same dreams adults do. They just don't have the ability to turn their dreams into reality."

"Are you a philosopher?" Dawn asked. Something about his tone told her he wasn't just looking for a way to change the subject.

"Sometimes. I'm just saying we all have dreams we have to let go of. I wanted to be a pro football player. It didn't turn out. I have to carve out another dream, one more in tune with reality."

Dawn had eaten all she wanted, but she wasn't ready for the evening to end. "What's that?" she asked.

"What's my dream? Let's call it a goal. That's a more realistic term. Dreams are for children. I want to turn this new franchise into a success for me as well as the men holding the purse strings. I've seen the possibility of the Rogue Valley joining the Northwest League for several years. I enjoy the challenge."

"I'd be scared of that kind of responsibility. You should have seen me when it was suggested I should apply for a supervisor's job. By then I knew I was a square peg stuck in a round hole. I belong out of doors, not behind a desk. I certainly wasn't cut out for a Chicago life-style. My roots were here, not in some huge city. What got you interested in the job with the league?"

"You're not the only one who felt it was time for a change in life, Dawn," Brian replied. "I was running a public relations business in Washington, but, well, let's just say that when I heard Verdue Field had been purchased by a major league franchise, I decided I wanted to become more closely involved in sports than I had in recent years. Washington wasn't right for me anymore. Like you, I have a certain fondness for the Rogue Valley. I went after the job and I got it. I think being a hometown product helped. The owners probably figured I knew my way around the county, had local connections. Now to see if they're right."

Dawn noted that Brian was still watching the small boy who was now sampling the croutons that had rolled to the edge of the salad bar. "How long have you been working for them?"

Brian stretched, yawned, and slowly got to his feet. "Long enough to have filled tomorrow with meetings. It's going to be a long day. What about you, Miss Morrell? The players will be arriving in a few days. I'm sure you want to be ready for them."

Dawn accepted his arm around her shoulders as they started toward the front door. For a moment she allowed herself to go back—back to that perfect night. She used to dream that she and the oh-so-popular Brian Riegel would be seen everywhere with their arms around each other and stars in their eyes. The other girls would have to deal with their jealousy. Dawn Morrell was the one he had chosen. But that was when she was a teenager filled with fantasy. They were years older now and there were no stars in their eyes.

"Thanks for the pizza. I'll have to get up early and jog it off," she admitted, feeling the need to end the evening on an impersonal note.

Brian stopped with his hand on the exit door. His arm was still on Dawn's shoulders, but his eyes were on the small crouton-eating boy. "He reminds me of my son," he said.

Chapter Three

Dawn had just returned from a three-mile run and was getting her things together for a shower when the doorbell rang. For a moment she told herself it could be Brian standing at the other side. But he'd dropped her off at her car at Verdue Field last night. He didn't even know where she lived.

The woman standing outside the door was an inch shorter than Dawn and perhaps fifteen pounds lighter, but except for those minor differences, Dawn found herself looking into her own future.

"What are you doing here, Mom?" Dawn gasped. "I'm sorry. Come on in. This is great. I was going to call you today." Dawn hugged her mother to her, feeling the frailty of the older woman. "I apologize for the way I look, but sweats really are the things to wear before the day comes up."

"You'll never convince me that a cup of coffee doesn't work as well as jogging to wake a person up," Crystal Morrell observed as the door closed. "I hope you don't mind my dropping by so early, but I had to see your place. I was afraid I'd make a nuisance of myself if I waited a few more days. I know you're going to be terribly busy when the ballplayers show!"

"So you've admitted I haven't been pulling your leg, have you?" Dawn teased as she guided her mother to her pride and joy—a comfortable old pillow of a chair she'd bought at a secondhand shop and reupholstered herself. "Your daughter really is going to be working with a bunch of jocks."

"My dear, there isn't much about you that surprises me. I used to think your brother was going to be the adventurous one, right up until the time he went to work for his father-in-law. Not you, though. You're the independent one. Aren't you going to give me the grand tour?"

"In a few minutes," Dawn assured her mother. "I want to hear what the doctor had to tell you. I can't believe you haven't had a checkup for five years." She shook her head. "Whatever would you do without me around to nag you?"

"I'm sure I don't know. I'm just delighted to have you back in this neck of the woods. But I hope you didn't do it because of me. I'll survive."

"I know you will, Mom. I'm here because I have this exciting new job. I just think it's nice that things worked out so we'll be living near each other." Her mom was thinner than Dawn would have liked her to be, but then there probably wasn't much incentive in cooking for one. At least she still carried herself with the air of a woman who was comfortable with who she was. Her once ash-colored hair was now silver, but it was still thick enough for a full style. "I think you're avoiding the question," Dawn pressed. "What did the doctor say?"

Crystal Morrell sighed. "He says I'm anemic. Two

hours of poking and prodding, to say nothing of a bill that's going to look like the national debt, and he says I need to take an iron supplement. I don't want to talk about that. What have you learned about your job?"

"I've learned I'm a little nervous about it. Mom, do you remember Brian Riegel? He was ahead of me in school." It seemed strange to be saying Brian's name to her mother. During that year—or was it more—when Dawn had her schoolgirl crush on Brian, she'd kept his identity a secret from her family. Feelings like that were too special to be subjected to dinnertime conversation. "We're going to be working together. He's the general manager."

"Brian Riegel? I'm afraid the name doesn't ring a bell. When did you meet with him?"

Briefly Dawn told her mother about the chance meeting at Verdue Field last night. They shared a laugh over Dawn's embarrassment at being caught giving in to a childhood fantasy. "I could have crawled into a hole and died! I was all caught up in my little bit of playacting. I had no idea anyone was watching me."

"What's he like? Do you think you're going to get along?"

"I don't know, Mom." Dawn considered glossing over her reaction to being around Brian, but admitted it was something she needed to talk out. "I keep getting yesterday and today confused in my mind when it comes to him. I remember him as a college jock. I think I may have put him on a bit of a pedestal in those days." She laughed. "It certainly was easy to do. I mean, all the girls my age were crazy about him. He was written up in the sports page several times and he was always being given some award or another during school assemblies. I remember when he crowned the homecoming queen and then took her to the senior prom. I thought the Brian Riegels of the world were beyond my reach. Now we're going to be working together."

Crystal Morrell took her daughter's hand. "Did you have a crush on him, dear?"

Dawn responded by laughing off the innocent, but too-probing question. "It was so long ago that I don't really remember. He looks older, but then so do I. We had a long talk last night."

"What about?"

"Work. I'm afraid he isn't convinced I can whip a bunch of jocks together. He probably thinks I'm in way over my head. I tried to explain what sports medicine is all about, but I'm not sure he was listening. I guess I'm just going to have to prove myself to him. If he remembers me at all, it's probably as a silly, giggling girl." Dawn stretched back in her own chair and then leaned forward. "How about that tour of the mansion? I have to show off the homestead to someone."

Dawn led her mother through the compact two-bedroom house she had bought. In the past Dawn had rented, but after looking at a dozen indistinguishable apartments, she admitted she'd come to the point in her life when she wanted a plot of land to call her own. The house was old enough that she probably should have had the wiring checked out, but there was a large fenced backyard with an apple tree and a gentle slope covered with strawberry plants. The steeply pitched roof contained an unfinished attic that could be converted into another bedroom. Living independently had at least given Dawn the opportunity to accumulate the type of furniture that fit into her life-style. There was nothing of an up-to-the-minute nature. Rather, Dawn was drawn to wood and durable fabrics. One of her most cherished pieces was a rolltop desk she'd picked up at an auction and spent countless hours refinishing. "I don't really need a desk," she told her mother. "But look at the grain in it. It's cherry. I couldn't pass it up."

Crystal looked around at the second bedroom, which, in addition to the large desk, contained Dawn's stereo, a recliner, her exercise mat, and a compact round trampoline. "What do you call this room?"

"I have no idea!" Dawn laughed. "It's kind of a catchall, isn't it? But I'll probably spend more time in it than in the living room. This place may never make the front cover of a decorating magazine, but I'm comfortable here."

"Dawn, are you sure this is what you want?"

Dawn knew what was behind her mother's question. "It is for now, Mom," she answered gently. "Fifteen years ago single women didn't buy their own homes, did they? They sat in their apartments and waited for Prince Charming to wisk them off to some ivy-covered cottage. But I'm afraid all the cottages are filled up these days. Either that or they've been turned into condominiums. I want permanence in my life. I'm tired of feeling as if my life is in limbo."

"But what about marriage?" Crystal took her daughter's hands. "I happen to remember a very romantic teenager. One of my greatest concerns was that you were going to run off and get married before you finished high school. I can't believe you've changed that much."

"I haven't. I still believe in love."

"Then why aren't you married? Oh, I'm sorry. I swore I wasn't going to do that. I have no right asking you that question."

"That's all right," Dawn reassured her mother. "If you don't have the right, who does? To tell you the truth, I don't know why I'm not married. It's not because I haven't been asked." She laughed to lighten the mood. "I don't think I'm all that hard to get along with. But the right man—for me—hasn't come along. Maybe I'm too picky. Maybe I should have stayed in Chicago and seen what might develop between Jim and me now that he's back on his feet. But I feel we were heading in an unhealthy direction. I was so relieved to see him recover, but I think we were both holding on to something that wasn't there."

"How is Jim?" Crystal had rushed to her daughter's side after the accident and during her stay while Dawn was in the hospital came to know Jim. "Has he gone back to work?"

Dawn nodded. "I had a long talk with the doctor in charge of his case before I made the decision to move. The doctor confirmed my suspicions. Jim has been relying on me too much. It's time to cut the cords."

"You don't love him, do you?"

"Oh, Mom, I don't know!" Dawn groaned. "Yes, I love him. But I don't know what label to put on the kind of love I feel for him. We went through a lot together. When I wasn't sure he'd ever walk again, every bit of emotional energy I had went toward trying to help him...." Dawn's voice trailed off as she slipped mentally into the past. "For a long time I don't think I existed outside the hospital. When he was up, I was too. And when he was depressed— But is that the kind of bond that should exist between a man and a woman?" Dawn shook her head. "I wish I knew the answer to that. The truth is, that's part of why I wanted this new job. I need some breathing space between Jim and me."

"Does Jim understand that?"

"He said he did. He's stronger emotionally than he was a few months ago. I think my getting away will speed his ability to fend for himself." Dawn shook her head again. "I don't want to spend all my time with you rehashing my problems. Are you sure the doctor didn't find anything wrong with you? You lost weight after Dad died." Dawn placed her hands on her mother's shoulders and stared into the older woman's eyes. "Are you sure you're taking your vitamins?"

"Yes ma'am." Crystal saluted sharply. "I'm being a good girl. I knew there'd be no end to your nagging if I wasn't. Besides"—she glanced at her watch—"I'm going to have to cut this visit short or I'll be late."

"Late? For what?"

"For work." Crystal laughed. "Not work, actually. Do you remember Peter Tinseth? He works in the district attorney's office. He and your father knew each other for years. Well, he's going to run for county commissioner. I've agreed to work on his campaign."

"That's wonderful! My mother, the politician."

"Not me," Crystal said as she reached for her

purse. "I'm content to work behind the scenes. But I must admit it's exciting to be in on Peter's campaign."

Dawn couldn't stop thinking about the glint in her mother's eyes after she'd closed the door behind the older woman. Peter Tinseth had divorced his wife years ago, and Dawn hadn't heard about any remarriage. Was there more to the relationship between the aspiring county commissioner and her mother than business? Dawn was relieved to realize that the thought didn't bother her. Her father was dead. Her mother had gone through a rough year since his death. She was entitled to some happiness in her life now.

You won't mind, will you Dad? Dawn thought as she walked into the bathroom and slipped out of her jogging outfit. *If Mom's happy, you're happy.*

And what about you, Dawn Morrell? Are you happy?

That question had no answer, at least none that came as she soaped her lean tanned body and rubbed shampoo through her hair. Dawn went through life with an upbeat philosophy. She suspected that some of it came from her determination to maintain a positive outlook. No matter how trying her day had been, a half hour of running restored her spirit and kept her body functioning as a well-oiled machine.

And yet her mother had hit on a simple, unescapable fact. Dawn was living alone. She had been an unbelievably romantic teenager. She'd been engaged twice while in college and dated a number of men since then. But none of those men ever turned her heart into a winged, soaring thing.

None. Not since Brian Riegel. He'd made her feel

as if she were swinging for the fence with the bases loaded and that nothing but the limits of her dreams could stop her from a home run.

That was the problem, Dawn admitted as she toweled off. She'd been too romantic as a teenager. Her heart had been a willing participant in the magic daydream she'd weaved about what life would be like if the football hero named Brian Riegel took her in his arms and held her through a moonlit night.

Well, he'd done that. Her wildest fantasies had come true in one magic, wondrous night.

Only there'd been just that one night.

Don't do this to yourself, Dawn chided herself. That was years ago. She wasn't a love-struck child anymore. Brian Riegel was a businessman. She was a nurse and a trainer. Magic nights and brilliant stars and a singing heart didn't really exist. They lived only in the all-too-susceptible mind of a girl who had fallen in love for the first time.

Brian Riegel never knew how she felt. And, over the years, she'd gotten over him.

Besides, he had a child.

Did Brian have a wife? Nothing he'd said last night gave any clue to the existence of a wife. He'd taken her out to dinner, held her head, put his arm around her, but maybe that was the way Brian treated all women. It was possible that the gestures meant nothing to him. A man as dynamic as Brian Riegel must be used to having women around him. He'd certainly never lacked for female companionship when he was in school. Was this how he kept a little spice in his life? That's all it was, an innocent touch. Brian didn't need anymore. He had a wife to go home to.

But did he? What were his words? *"He reminds me of my son."* It sounded as if Brian didn't see his child all the time.

Stop it! Dawn glared at herself in the mirror, oblivious of the tan that was the envy of most of the people she knew. *You and Brian Riegel have a business relationship. Stop trying to probe into his personal life.*

Dawn had slipped into a short terry coverup and was padding barefoot into the kitchen to fix herself breakfast when the doorbell rang.

"What'd you forget, Mom?" she called out, flinging open the door.

It wasn't her mother. "Your hair's wet," Brian Riegel observed.

Dawn stepped back. "My mother was just here. I thought she'd forgotten something."

"You're just lucky I'm not a door-to-door salesman," Brian observed. He was dressed for work, tan trousers and a cream knit pullover replacing the casual clothes of yesterday. He shook his head, grinning slightly. "You'd probably scare off the poor fellow."

"Do I look that bad?" Dawn hadn't applied any makeup after her shower, but then she seldom did. A little eye shadow and mascara maybe, but her skin didn't need added color and she didn't believe in blocking off her pores.

Brian cocked his head to one side as if seriously considering the question. "Your toes aren't anything spectacular, but then toes are more utilitarian than glamorous, aren't they? The legs aren't bad. Calves more muscular than most women's, but I understand that's one of the by-products of jogging. That's quite a fetching outfit."

Dawn pulled down on the hem of her coverup. Underneath she was wearing bikini underpants and nothing else. "Uh, do you mind? I'll run and get dressed."

Brian stopped her. "Don't bother. Actually, I just dropped by to deliver a short message. I won't be long."

"Oh." Did she really want him to leave? she wondered. His comment about her legs, rather than embarrassing her, gave her secret pleasure. She'd never apologized for her taut calves. "How did you find out where I live?"

"I have my ways," Brian said mysteriously, rubbing his chin dramatically. "Actually, it was simple. I looked it up in the personnel file. I like your taste in houses."

Dawn flushed at the compliment. "So do I. The neighborhood is what they call mixed, I believe, but the trees have been around long enough that kids can actually climb them. I don't know why anyone would choose to live where everything green is stuck in little planters. Won't you come in? You don't have to stand in the doorway."

Brian closed the door behind him. The move had brought him a step closer, and Dawn stepped back instinctively, thrown off-balance by his nearness. "I thought your hair was almost white," he observed. "It's kind of silver now."

"That's because it's wet," Dawn managed, running a nervous finger through the wet strands. "I don't like to blow-dry it because it winds up looking like I put my finger in a light socket."

"It's such an unusual color."

"Yes." The subject was innocent enough. Why was

she having so much trouble keeping her wits about her? she wondered. "My father's hair was the same color. Mom's is light too. The poor man. I guess he was teased about it when he was a child. People accept unusual hair color on a woman, not on a man."

"Too bad newspapers only print black-and-white pictures." He reached out and touched her hair.

"What are you talking about?" she asked, forcing herself not to retreat from his unsettling touch. "What does my hair have to do with newspapers?"

"I'm setting up an interview with you and the sports reporter of the *Nugget*." Brian smiled briefly. "I must say he's eager to meet the team's trainer, especially when I told him you were a woman. A young woman."

Was Brian using her? she wondered. The thought had entered her mind last night and now it was coming back. "Don't you think you should have checked with me before making such arrangements? Maybe I don't want to be interviewed."

"Do you want to have a job next year?"

"What? Of course. Is that a threat?" They were still standing near the front door, Dawn holding her coverup together, Brian with a briefcase in his left hand, but Dawn wasn't thinking about inviting him to sit down.

"Hardly. Financial facts of life." Brian emphasized his point by tapping his forehead. "This farm team has to be self-supporting. And it is self-supporting only if we draw enough fans into the stands—paying fans. Part of my job is to generate interest in the team and its members, even its trainer. Dawn, you're an asset to the organization."

"An asset? Is that how you see me? You don't care a bit about my real job, do you?" she challenged, forgetting that a moment ago she'd been responding to Brian in a most unsettling way. "If I was old and fat, you'd let me go quietly about my job, but you'd hardly glance in my direction. You certainly wouldn't set up an interview with the newspaper."

"Probably not," he observed. "Be realistic, Dawn. I have a job to do for the organization. I'm determined to do the best I'm capable of. A mature employee would be aware of that."

"Oh, I'm mature enough all right. That's what usually happens when you've been supporting yourself for a number of years. Is that what you came here for? To tell me to play the game according to your rules when the reporter comes to interview me?"

"I was hoping I wouldn't have to spell it out. Actually, I have something I'd like to get your opinion on." He stepped around her and went over to the living room couch. He'd sat down and was opening his briefcase when he again spoke. "You grew up around Verdue Field," he said without looking at her. "I've written a piece on the field's background. It's going to appear in the brochure I'm putting together to be distributed at home games. I'd like to get your reaction before I send it to the printer."

Dawn forced aside her emotions and joined Brian on the couch. He was right. Theirs was a business relationship. She was mistaken to try to read anything more into it. After all, they were both little more than children when they'd had their one night together.

"I practically grew up there," Dawn explained, sitting far enough way from Brian so she wouldn't have to worry about her body's strange response to him. "I can't remember how old I was when they put in the new seats."

"Read." Brian dropped the sheets of typing in her lap. "Tell me what you think."

"Right now? You want me to read this while you wait?"

"Of course. I need to get it to the printer today. You don't have to go anywhere right now, do you?"

"No. Not really." She wanted to have a look at the training facilities, but that could wait until later in the day. Dawn turned her attention to what Brian had written.

The story that unfolded about Verdue Field was done in a gentle, almost poetic tone. The facts and figures regarding the complex's background were skillfully woven into the body of the work, which managed to make Verdue Field more than grass and concrete and wood and fencing. Brian had captured the diamond's essence, stirred Dawn's memories, made her want to hurry over and once again breathe in the sweet scent of freshly mowed grass.

The roots of Verdue Field had begun almost a century ago. The land was originally owned by the son of a Spanish family that had begun one of the pear orchards that were still partially responsible for the economic health of the valley. Roberto Mendez had set aside one section of his family's vast holdings. Instead of planting fruit trees, he'd cleared the land and then fought to keep the city from engulfing it. Two years before his death he'd deeded the acreage to the county with the stipulation that it remain exclusively for recreational use. Once in the hands of the county, the land had been entrusted to the parks and recreation department. Fortunately, Steven Harper, a man who'd known the Mendez family, was then at the head of parks and recreation. He headed the drive to turn the unimproved acres into a sports complex. Improvements took place slowly over a period of many years, but now Verdue Field, named for its rich green outfields, was the pride of the Rogue Valley. The county had offered Verdue Field to any baseball organization in need of playing space. In the past it had been used exclusively by nonprofit organizations, but the economy in recent years was such that the county decided it was time for Verdue Field to generate its own revenue.

It had been offered to a number of professional baseball franchises as playing space for one of their farm teams. Now the county had a contract with the A's in hand. Young men with dreams of becoming professional ballplayers would soon be playing on Roberto Mendez's land.

"It's perfect," Dawn breathed, eyes sparkling. "The way you've written it, Verdue Field has come to life. It isn't just acres of grass with base paths marked on it. People are going to want to see it for themselves."

"That's the response I was hoping for. I had a devil of a time writing that thing. I wanted more than facts and figures, but I didn't want to romanticize it too much either."

"You've struck the right balance." Dawn allowed herself to meet Brian's eyes. "If I didn't know any better, I'd think you were a frustrated poet, not just a businessman."

"I wouldn't know about that. I know very little about poetry. There's nothing you think should be changed?"

Dawn shook her head. "Take it to the printer. There's life in Verdue Field. People will read this and see that."

"I thought about adding that I spotted you running the bases, but then I decided that might give other people the same idea."

Dawn refused to back down from the challenge in his eyes. "Maybe you should ask me to turn in my keys. You can't tell when I might do something like that again."

"I trust you." He was quiet for a minute. "There's something I want to clear up with you. Last night, when we were talking, you brought up our—shall we call it a date? I'm afraid I gave you the impression it had minimal impact on me. That was a misconception."

"Oh." For the life of her, Dawn couldn't grasp at a thing to say. His eyes were saying much more than his words, letting her know that the memory was vivid to him. Did he remember her total innocence, her total surrender, in his arms? Did he think she was still the same girl? Was this Brian's way of letting her know he was willing to pick up the threads of a single night?

Brian rose to his feet in a smooth motion that denied the existence of any surgery-scarred knees. "It was one of those experiences that should happen at least once to everyone."

"Brian?" She followed him blindly to the door. "It was a long time ago."

"Yes, it was." He turned to her. "But what happened that night was right. Very right. I don't regret it. Do you?''

She didn't answer him. Indeed, she couldn't have given him her name if her life depended on it. Brian — the man who turned a child into a woman. They'd shared too much to simply shake hands and call their relationship a business venture.

"Don't worry, Dawn. I've never told anyone what happened that night. I won't now. It's done. Finished. We're not the same people we were then.''

He was gone, taking the essence of life from the room with him. Shaken and weak, Dawn stumbled until she collapsed on the couch that still retained the warmth of Brian's body. He could have taken her in his arms and she wouldn't have resisted. Surely he sensed that.

But he hadn't touched her. He'd acknowledged their one night of romance but then dropped it as a finished chapter.

Today they were companions in a business venture. Nothing more. The past was dead.

Don't be a fool! Dawn chided herself. Again she surged to her feet, ripping off her coverup as she hurried into her bedroom, where her clothes waited. *You're the fool who won't let the memories die.* Hadn't Brian spelled out the ground rules? He was engaged in managing the business end of the organization they worked for. She was a financial asset, a drawing card, so to speak.

At least he was honest about that. Dawn yanked a top over her head and straightened the thin straps on her shoulders. The top fit loosely enough that her breasts weren't too sharply outlined. He hadn't told her what he considered appropriate wearing apparel, but she'd been able to read the unspoken message. She was to present herself as an attractive female, competent and self-assured but with a gentle hint of sensuality. A woman. Cleats were definitely not in order.

All right. She'd fit in as she was expected to. Brian wasn't interested in reviving the past. She'd take her clues from him, she decided.

Dawn was still asking herself whether she was capable of living up to everything Brian expected of her when her newly installed telephone rang. It was the sports reporter from the *Nugget*, Ralph Mercer. Would Dawn be able to meet him at Verdue Field in about two hours for an interview? he inquired. He wanted to take pictures too. He had nothing specific in mind, but it would come to him in the course of the interview. "Don't worry about it, kid. I've been throwing questions at people for years. I'll figure out what makes you tick."

Feeling a little nervous about having to answer a stranger's questions, Dawn agreed to the suggested time and then hung up. Was Brian going to be part of the interview, or would the article concentrate on her? Dawn had to admit she would prefer being woven into the fabric of a larger story centering around Verdue Field, but Brian had made it clear that any and all promotion of the baseball season would be to the organization's benefit. Dawn knew she was being used, but there didn't appear to be anything she could do about it.

But if Brian thought she was going to come across an an empty-headed acquisition brought in for sex appeal, he was going to be sadly mistaken. As Dawn got ready to leave for the field she mentally organized what she was going to say to the reporter. Her study in sports medicine following the healing of her broken leg gave her confidence. She was determined to make her point about sports conditioning and the proper level of training that would hold sports-related injuries to a minimum. So she looked like a refugee from the California surf. That didn't mean she had to sound like one.

Dawn had given herself enough time to tour the training facilities before her meeting with the reporter. With the keys she had been given she let herself into the deserted complex and walked to the building behind the home team dugout. Part of the building was given up to some kind of office, but around back was an area set aside for ballplayers. Dawn reminded herself that up until a few weeks ago Verdue Field hadn't been considered "home" for any ball club, but she couldn't help but be disappointed by what she saw. The dressing area was small and dark with barely enough room in it for players to hang their street clothes while dressing for a game. There was no separate, even minimally equipped training area, a situation Dawn was determined to take up with the general manager at the earliest opportunity.

At least someone had installed several weight benches, and weight lifting equipment of various vintages was piled in a corner of an area that apparently was currently being used for storage. It was hardly what the New York Yankees were accustomed to, but it would have to do until Dawn could present a budget for the organization to consider. She'd been told that she would be starting from scratch. Well, she could hardly argue that point.

What would the reaction be when she laid down the law—no amphetamines. Hopefully that wouldn't cause a problem, because that was one area where Dawn would allow no compromise. As long as she was around, the young athletes weren't going to take chances because of a desire to push themselves beyond a healthy, natural limit.

She was shaking her head at the sad remains of a first aid kit when she heard a masculine voice echoing off the empty stands. Dawn put down the metal box and stepped outside, grateful for the warmth of the sun on her skin following the time she'd spent in the cool building. It wasn't hard to recognize the tall man in his early forties as a reporter, standing just inside the gate she'd left open. He carried a camera slung over his slightly sloping shoulder. A notebook was tucked under his right arm.

"I believe you're looking for me," Dawn said.

The reporter moved his eyes slowly and boldly down Dawn's body before answering. "Riegel said I was going to be pleasantly surprised. I had no idea it was going to be this good."

"I hope you don't mind if we get down to business. The players are due in two days, and I have a great deal of work to do to prepare for them." The nerve of that man! What gave him the right to look at her as if she were a filly he was contemplating buying? Dawn knew that it was going to take a great deal of patience to keep from telling the man that she wanted nothing to do with him. But she didn't dare do that. He'd probably wind up writing that the

A's female trainer was uncooperative, a statement that certainly wouldn't help her job security.

"You're the boss, honey," he drawled. "Too bad you're in a hurry, though. I could spend the whole day with you. The night too."

Silently Dawn led the way to the front row of the grandstand and sat down, groaning because he seemed to find it necessary to sit with his knee touching her thigh. "I've never been interviewed before," she admitted. "I'm not sure what you want to know. Just so you don't have to ask, I do know the difference between a baseball and a football."

"Are you married?"

"What does that have to do with what I'm doing?" Dawn bit back the rest of her sharp retort. He was probably just baiting her. She was going to have to be very careful of what she said to him. "No, I'm not married," she relented.

"That's good. Real good." He grabbed her left hand and studied it briefly. "No ring. You're not engaged or anything?"

"No. I'm not engaged. Please, Mr. Mercer, I don't see what my marital state has to do with this interview."

"Call me Ralph. My wife calls me something else, but we don't want to go into that. Don't take it personal, Dawn, but when people see your picture, they're going to see an attractive young woman with a mop of white hair. They're going to be interested in you as a person. A little sex appeal sells newspapers, to say nothing of tickets. Okay." He leaned even closer. "Shoot. Tell me all about how you got into this line of work."

Dawn stumbled somewhat, finding it hard to form the words to explain how she'd gone from a high pressure hospital job to what she was jumping into now. She didn't want to tell Ralph about Jim and the accident. That was personal "I guess you can say I was ready for a change in my life;" she offered. "I love medicine, but I've never been happy working inside. Chicago doesn't have elbow room. I grew up surrounded by pear orchards, not skyscrapers. This was the best way I could find for getting back out into the fresh air."

"You can say that again." Ralph exhaled his cigarette-tainted breath in her direction. "You sure as hell don't look like someone who spent much time inside. Or sitting either. You're one of those physical fitness nuts, aren't you?"

"I suppose you could say that." Dawn didn't know whether Ralph meant his observation as a compliment or criticism. "I run regularly. And I exercise every day. I believe everyone should keep as physically fit as possible. That's why I'm excited about my job. I'll be working with young men whose success depends on physical fitness."

Before Dawn could react, Ralph had grabbed her upper arm and was exploring it roughly with his tobacco-stained fingers. "No big, bulging muscles. At least you're not one of those women who are into bodybuilding. No man likes a woman to look like she could beat him in arm wrestling."

"Ralph." Dawn tried to jerk away, but he held on. "I'd really like to concentrate on making my point about conditioning and sports medicine, not the state of my muscles."

Ralph grinned, showing darkened teeth. "We'll get back to the state of your muscles later. Okay, go ahead. Give me your speech." He released her arm and returned, reluctantly it seemed to Dawn, to his pencil and notebook.

Slowly at first, but with more confidence and enthusiasm as she saw that Ralph was taking notes, Dawn launched into her subject. She talked knowledgeably about the need for outlining a specific training program for every athlete. "It's essential for baseball players to be quick and strong. I'm not interested in developing them into muscle men, but they have to have good upper body strength, in addition to strong legs. We'll be concentrating on using muscles against resistance in the same manner they'll be used during competition."

"You sound like you know what you're talking about."

"I better. That's what I'm being paid for. It's a subject that turns me on." Dawn stopped, aghast at the slip of the tongue that might be misinterpreted. The taunt in Ralph's lazy eyes told her he hadn't missed a thing.

"Speed's essential for a ballplayer," Dawn hurried on, hoping her nervousness didn't show. She'd said essentially the same thing during her job interview, and that helped her now. "An athlete can't do anything about the potential he's born with, but there's a great deal he can do to reach his maximum ability. We'll be working on maximizing the performance of muscle fibers through specific training techniques. Fast running has been proved to develop what are known as fast twitch fingers. I'm working on a running schedule designed to help the players reach their peak. Because I want them to understand why they're doing specific exercises, I'll be giving them a cram course in sports medicine.''

"Do you really think they're going to be interested? Look, you're working with guys just out of school. Those young studs' hormones are working at maximum at that age. That's what they're going to be thinking about, especially if their trainer is a young woman in a formfitting top.''

Dawn bristled. Couldn't Ralph think of anything else? "If they want to play professionally, they'll listen,'' she snapped. "Those men you're talking about have worked hard to get as far as they are. They know what sacrifice is about.''

"I hope you're right, honey. Personally, I'm a lot more interested in finding out what it takes to get you between the sheets than what you know about twitch muscles.''

Dawn sprang to her feet. "You'll never know that!'' she snapped, her fingernails itching to bury themselves in the reporter's sagging cheeks. He was impossible! She was a breath away from giving him a tongue-lashing that he wouldn't soon forget.

"Calm down, honey.'' Ralph grabbed at her wrist and missed, raking his hand down her right thigh. "Don't tell me you haven't been teased before. You better get used to it. After all, you're definitely going to be a minority once those young bucks get here. A very alluring minority, I might point out.''

"I'm older than most of them. I expect them to respect me,'' Dawn pointed out through clenched teeth. No matter how much her job meant, she wasn't going to put up with this. "I hardly think that's going to be much of a problem."

"Don't be so sure of that. You're not over the hill. Not by a long shot."

Dawn took a long deep breath, willing herself to keep her temper in check. For all she knew, the whole conversation was a huge joke, with Ralph determined to throw her off-balance. Maybe this was no more than his way of gaining the upper hand in an interview. "I appreciate the compliment," she said, managing a smile she didn't feel. "May I ask you a question? You mentioned something I feel I have to comment on. Do you really think there's going to be a problem with the players relating to me as a trainer? Surely they're going to expect more from me than simply providing them with clean towels."

Ralph blinked before speaking. "That, my dear, is entirely up to you. If you act like a professional, they'll have no choice but to view you as one. However, if you keep on reminding them that you're a woman, you're going to have a battle on your pretty little hands. And short of wearing oversize sweat shirts, I don't know how you're going to avoid that." The challenge in Ralph's eyes was unmistakable.

"I appreciate your candor," Dawn said, easing herself back down near, but not too near, Ralph. "I assure you, it's something I've spent time thinking about. I admit that a female trainer is still a bit of a rarity, but I don't see why it should represent an insurmountable obstacle. After all, if the parent organization thought enough of my qualifications to hire me, I must have something going for me."

"Oh, you do. You do indeed, my dear." Again

Ralph's eyes made their lazy way down Dawn's body.

Trembling with indignation, Dawn forced the conversation back to its original intent. "I'm glad you agree. I've certainly worked hard enough educating myself. Let me give you an example. Sports medicine myths are something I intend on dispelling. I won't be surprised to find that a number of the athletes were brought up believing that the more protein they eat, the better off they'll be. Actually, steak is a poor source of immediate energy, and energy is what they need during a game. Worse than that, a steak laced with fat can actually impair performance. Fat takes a long time to digest. I'm going to be stressing carbohydrates. Of course, nothing can take the place of a balanced diet, but the point I'm trying to make is that the food components found in carbohydrates are the primary source of energy during vigorous exercise."

"What about sex?"

"What?"

"Do you advocate absention before a game? What about a player burning himself out in bed and having nothing left for the diamond?"

"That's an old superstition and I believe you know it," Dawn managed through clenched teeth. Talk about a one-track mind! "If a person is physically fit, he has more interest in sex. There's no reason why he should cut back in that activity." There. That should have shown Ralph that she wasn't going to shy away from the subject.

"In other words, you're going to encourage the players to go out and look for sex." Ralph was bent over his notebook and was writing quickly.

Dawn envisioned finding that misinterpretation of

what she said in print and cringed. "Don't put words in my mouth. That's not what I said. What I want to see in print, if you really believe the topic needs to be made public at all, is that it takes more energy for pregame warm-ups than for sexual relations."

Ralph looked disappointed. "That's not exactly earth-shattering news."

"I don't see any reason why it should be." Dawn allowed herself a secret smile. Poor Ralph wasn't getting anywhere, was he? "Can't you just do a straight story on me? Why does sex have to be part of it?"

"Because you're a sexy young woman." Ralph's grin was positively evil. "One more question. What about you? Do you believe that sex is a desirable form of exercise? Are you in the habit of making the bed part of your physical fitness program?"

"That, Mr. Mercer, is none of your business."

Ralph shrugged but continued to grin. "I'd certainly hate to think that this topic was closed. It's certainly a lot more interesting than carbohydrates. I'll tell you what. How about I take my pictures and then the two of us go somewhere for a drink?"

Dawn didn't know whether to be angry or laugh off his suggestion. "What about your wife? Don't you think we should ask her along?"

"What wife? Did I mention a wife? Come off it, Dawn. What's wrong with our spending a little time together? No one has to know."

"I'd know." Dawn rose to her feet, no longer caring whether Ralph Mercer wrote anything about her or not. She just wanted to get away from the man. "You said you wanted to take a picture. Where do you want me to stand?"

"I don't want you standing anywhere. I'm trying to get you into the prone position, if you haven't noticed." Ralph took a step toward Dawn.

She stepped back, alarm surging through her body. Was he playing games or serious? "And if you haven't noticed, I'm trying to tell you that I'm not interested. I'm sure you have other things to do. So do I."

Ralph only laughed, his beefy hands reaching for her. "No, you don't," he said, his voice a menacing growl. "Do I have to spell it out, Miss Morrell? This game is being played in my ball park. I can say anything in the article that I want to. You be nice to me, and the piece will be everything your employers could want. Give me a hard time, and they're going to start wondering whether they made a mistake by hiring you."

Dawn got the message. Because she was so intent on trying to think of something to say, she didn't spring back when Ralph put his hands on her shoulders. She stood looking up at him, hating everything about him. "You have no right!"

"You're right about that, young lady. I have absolutely no right." He brought his lips within an inch of hers. "However, I'm doing it."

"Don't." Dawn tried to twist out of his grasp, reluctant to make a scene if there was any way of appealing to his sense of reason. "What if I say something to your editor?"

"Like what? I haven't done anything—yet. I haven't torn your clothes off you or forced you into a compromising position. As far as I know, there's no law against a little kiss." His lips bore down on hers, shutting off anything she might have said.

Dawn's body went rigid as Ralph's hard lips sealed themselves against hers, his body pushing hard against her legs, her waist, her breasts. There was no hint of response from her. Indeed, response was the last thing in the world that would have occurred to her. Even as she fought to escape his actions she doubted that rape was on his mind. Ralph obviously believed that his threat of a slanted article was all it would take to bring her around.

Well, that was the last thing she'd ever consider! Ralph was disgusting, an obnoxious man with only one thing on his mind. She didn't care how many times his threat of blackmail had worked to his advantage. It was going to backfire this time. "Don't!" she hissed, whipping her head to one side to escape the loathsome contact. "I'll tell—"

"Who are you going to tell?" he challenged, leaning over and forcing her off-balance. "There's no one here but you and me."

"You're wrong about that."

Dawn's legs went weak at the unexpected words. They weren't alone! She wouldn't have to fight Ralph off singlehandedly. As Ralph released his grip on her, Dawn turned in the direction of the masculine voice.

Brian Riegel was standing spread-legged in the aisle leading to the bleachers. He was wearing the same clothes he'd worn to her place this morning, but he looked bigger somehow. Dawn's relief at his appearance was total. She reached toward the back of the seat she'd vacated to steady herself, admitting that fear had been laced in with her anger.

Brian's eyes were on her. "Did I interrupt something? If I did, I'll apologize. But from where I stood the embrace looked rather one-sided."

"It was!" Dawn gasped, not stopping to ask herself why she was so determined that Brian not misinterpret what he'd witnessed. "I didn't agree to it in the slightest."

Ralph turned on her. "That's your story, Miss Morrell. Why don't you let me tell my side of it. You come on wearing that little bit of nothing for a top and expect me to pretend you're not sending out little messages? After all, I'm only human."

Dawn gasped at the absurdity of what Ralph was saying. Seduction was the last thing she'd had on her mind when she agreed to the interview. "That's the most ridiculous—"

Brian interrupted. "Is the interview over?"

Ralph shrugged. He'd picked up his note pad and pencil and once again struck the pose of the seasoned reporter. "Except for the pictures."

"Then I suggest you get on with it," Brian said curtly. "I have business to discuss with Miss Morrell."

Dawn submitted to Ralph's suggestions regarding pictures for the article, not because she wanted anything more to do with him but because she was determined to show him that his behavior hadn't shaken her self-confidence. She did as she was told, first posing alongside a rack of bats and then standing along the left field foul line as if demonstrating the proper stance to begin wind sprints. Ralph took several close-ups and then started packing away his equipment. "The article will be in tomorrow night's paper. I hope you'll buy a copy."

"I wouldn't miss it for the world," Dawn said. "I'm curious to see if you were listening." Her large blue eyes narrowed. "It will be an objective article, won't it?"

"I'm a professional. I know what I'm doing."

Silence settled over the grandstand after Ralph left. Now that the reporter was no longer around, Dawn found herself giving in to a delayed reaction to the humility he'd subjected her to. She still didn't believe she'd been in any physical danger, but his arrogance enraged her. What made him think—even remotely—that he had the right to kiss her, to press his body against hers! she raged. She was a far cry from some slave at his beck and call. And yet he'd tried to do as he wanted with her. "That man!" she fumed, her voice shaky despite her attempt to calm her nerves. "I still can't believe it. I was so surprised, I didn't do anything."

"Is that what it was? I was watching. You didn't slap him or scream or have any of the traditional reactions."

Dawn turned on Brian. Was there a hint of criticism in his voice? she wondered. "Would it make you feel better if I had? How about if I had hit him with a body block? Maybe I could have slid into him with my cleats up."

"It seems to me that would be preferable to doing nothing."

"I'm glad you're able to reduce everything to simple standards of right and wrong," Dawn said, shaken because she didn't like the direction the conversation was taking. She wanted him to pat her hand and tell her everything was all right, not hold her at arm's length. Didn't he realize she needed him on her side? "I've never been manhandled like that before. I'm sure if I had, I'd have been better at reacting in what you consider an acceptable fashion."

"Actually, I'm not very interested in what you did or didn't do and why. How you conduct yourself is your own business. As long as you don't do anything to put the organization in a bad light, you're free to live your own life."

Dawn felt as if she'd been slapped. "That's a relief!" she shot back. "I'd hate to think I have to check with you every time I turn around."

"It put all of us in an awkward position. I hope it doesn't happen again."

"It won't. I have no intention of seeing Ralph Mercer ever again."

"That's your business." Brian had turned away and was starting to walk back toward the entrance to Verdue Field.

Dawn stared at his hard back. She'd just seen a side of Brian she didn't know existed. He'd been rather remote back when they were in high school, but that, Dawn suspected, was only because she was too in awe of him to get to know him as a human being. Now, however, he didn't seem to care anything about her. It wasn't fair! she thought. She hadn't done anything to deserve this.

"Brian? I'm grateful to you for stepping in. Is that what you want me to say? What have I done wrong?"

He whirled on her. "You haven't done anything wrong. Let's just say I have questions about your qualifications to adequately represent the organization we both work for. You're a woman in a field dominated by men. I'd have thought you'd have realized that by now."

She shook her head angrily. "You say I haven't done anything wrong, but now you're questioning my qualifications. You're contradicting yourself."

"Am I?" He was facing her fully now, the strength in his jaw reflected in the way he carried himself, the way his eyes refused to give any quarter. "I can't tell you how to conduct yourself, Dawn. But it should be clear that as far as the press is concerned, you're a trainer first and a woman second. Ralph may have an overactive imagination, but he had to receive some kind of message from you that he perceived as a green light."

"That's ridiculous!" Dawn grasped her hands together, her shoulders actually quivering from the force of her emotions. "I didn't do—say—anything. Ralph disgusts me."

"I'm not the slightest bit interested in what you think of Ralph. In fact, the less I hear from you about your opinions regarding the male sex, the better. I've had quite enough of that in my life, thank you."

Dawn opened her mouth but nothing came out. Like his brief comment about a son, this momentary glimpse into Brian's personal life came and went too quickly for her to fully comprehend it. "Brian, please believe me," she whispered. "I didn't do anything to encourage him. I can't help being a woman."

"I know that, Dawn."

Chapter Four

Dawn should have had no trouble falling asleep. After a full day spent at Verdue Field, making final preparations to receive the eighteen ballplayers expected the next morning, she'd changed into running shoes and shorts and laced an unplanned path through the city's night-quietened streets. She preferred jogging when she could be assured of minimum competition from cars, not only because it made her uneasy to have to be on the lookout for them but because her years in Chicago made her deeply appreciative of what she termed her breathing space. Her run took her past several schools where groups of youngsters and men had gathered for baseball or softball practice. Football season resulted in fever pitch excitement in the fall as the city's high school team fought its way to one state championship after another. But it was in the spring that athletics—or rather baseball—brought the county to life. Somewhere Dawn had read that the Rogue Valley had a higher percentage of people playing on diamonds than anywhere else in the country. From her vantage point as she jogged around newly mowed fields, she could well believe the distinction.

Baseball was big in the Rogue Valley. People both young and old, weary of late winter and early spring rains, sought the out-of-doors in programs of physical activity. It didn't hurt to have had a fast pitch softball team go to the national finals twice in the past three years.

And it certainly wouldn't hurt to bring professional baseball to the valley. Converting Verdue Field into a paying enterprise was sure to be rewarded with fans willing to pay the nominal fee it took to be able to watch aspiring all-stars in action.

Following her run, Dawn showered and then settled down to a light supper and the evening paper. Despite her earlier apprehension, Ralph's article was a straightforward piece with no cute references to Dawn's youth or minority status in a male-dominated field. She considered calling Ralph to thank him for his objectivity but decided against it. It probably wouldn't take much to convince Ralph that her phone call was a subtle suggestion that their relationship continue beyond that of interviewer and interviewee.

At least I don't have to worry about Ralph giving his readers a false impression of me, Dawn thought as she slipped between lavender sheets, her window opened to catch the clean scent of spring night air.

But sleep didn't come. Although she fought it, Brian Riegel attacked her thoughts, her senses. He'd said very little to her today. In fact, she'd seen him for only a few minutes as he was showing a radio sportscaster around the broadcasting booth. He'd been intent on the matter at hand, easily answering questions about the availability of biographical material on the players, sidelights on the grounds keeping crew, and several promotional campaigns he was developing designed to aid youth athletics. Obviously, his years in public relations were working to his benefit these days. Dawn had been impressed with Brian's grasp of the total program, his innate business sense.

But tonight she thought of him as a man.

Brian had changed from those innocent years when their futures had been as limitless as their dreams. Dawn remembered an interview the school newspaper had done on Brian in conjunction with an upcoming homecoming football game. He'd spoken of his college career majoring in architecture, followed, he felt sure, by contracts with a professional football team and unlimited years pulling in passes on the field.

It doesn't turn out the way we think it will, does it, Brian? Dawn thought as she shifted position, trying to still her restless muscles. One tackle with a linebacker's helmet grinding into your knee and it's all over, she knew.

A lesser man might have given up, buried himself in lost dreams, and gone through the rest of his life only half alive. But not Brian. He'd had the necessary surgery, turned in his uniform, and gone about channeling his life in another direction. He hadn't attained the star status she'd thought was his due when she was too young to have faced reality, but she could be proud of the man he'd turned into.

And yet there was no denying that she really didn't know him anymore. There was a past—a child—he wasn't ready to trust her with yet. But he held his head high, moved with confidence in the business world, and was helping shape the future of young men who now carried the dreams that had once been his.

What about you, Brian? What are your dreams? What do you want that you don't have in your life? Why is this barrier between us, this feeling that I'm being held at arm's length? Is is just me, or are you part of that barrier too?

Why should she care?

Dawn pushed her feet down to the bottom of her bed and repositioned her arms. She'd spent over a year totally involved with Jim, helping him get his life back on course. What did she need with another involvement? Brian was no longer the handsome youth she'd been so deeply, so totally in love with. That love belonged to innocent youth, not the reality of adulthood. Because the night afforded no distractions, she had to face the fact that the football hero she'd carried in her dreams might not have ever existed.

And yet the memory remained. That one night in Brian Riegel's arms made all other nights in her life pale by comparison.

The fact was, she wasn't going to go to the party when her best friend, April Stevens, told her about the bash the college football team was throwing. "It's open to everyone," April had said when she caught Dawn in the hall between classes. "Especially attractive high-school girls."

"I bet," Dawn replied warily. "Those jocks would like nothing better than to be surrounded by admiring females. We probably wouldn't be able to get within ten feet of any of them."

"We'll never know if we don't go. Come on. Brian will be there. He's all you've talked about for months

You've been in a blue funk ever since he graduated from high school. What good has it done you to sit in the stands? He couldn't see you up there. He'd have to notice you if you're in the same room with him."

"I don't know." It wasn't that she didn't want to go. Her heart was skipping wildly with the thought of breathing the same air Brian did. But what if he didn't look her way? What if he was with another girl? Could she stand the pain? she asked herself. "I don't know what to wear to a college party."

"Clothes, you dope. The guys will take one look at that white hair of yours and won't even think to look at what you're wearing. I don't believe it! You help your folks in their garden and you get a better tan than I had lifeguarding all summer. It's disgusting!" April ran her fingers through her own short dark curls. "Look, if I can go looking like a mouse that got caught in permanent wave solution I don't know what your problem is. Why don't you wear your white outfit? That new number will really make them sit up and take notice."

Dawn had laughed. The outfit had been April's idea, and April hadn't forgiven her friend for not wearing it yet. "I look like Casper the Friendly Ghost in that. Just one white mass."

"For crying out loud! You look like a floating angel in it." April shook her head. "I don't know why you won't listen to me. I have fantastic taste in clothes—at least when it comes to picking out clothes for you. I don't know why you won't admit you look like a Miss America candidate in that white sweater. It shows off curves I won't have if I do exercises all my life."

April knew all about Dawn's love-hate affair with

her pale hair, so there was no need going over that. She always had to be careful not to damage it with chemicals and the sun and had given up on trying to get it to curl. "Brian doesn't know I'm alive," she moaned.

April groaned back, imitating her friend's mournful tone. "And he never will as long as you keep on staring at him from a distance. Girl, I don't believe you. Brian's the only boy you've been interested in, isn't he? Here's your chance. You've been moping around ever since he went to college. Are you going to spend the rest of the year dreaming about him, or are you going to go after him?"

Dawn shuddered at the thought of going after Brian. All she wanted was for him to notice her, to want to talk to her. To—just once in her life—take her in his arms.

After that? Dawn's dreams hadn't gone beyond the magic of finding herself in Brian Riegel's embrace.

In the end Dawn went, holding April's hand for courage. The two girls arrived at the huge old house, which housed a half dozen college males, after most of the others were already dancing to the music blaring from someone's stereo. They'd barely stepped inside when someone thrust foaming glasses of beer in their hands and they were challenged to "drink up and enjoy."

Dawn stood in an unoccupied corner, staring out at the long dark hallway leading to high-ceilinged rooms. Already April was deep in conversation with the big redhead who'd handed them their drinks. Dawn stared at the glass in her hand and then took a tentative sip. Bubbles tickled her nose; the liquid going down her throat made her shudder. She took another swallow and decided she simply wasn't cut out to be a beer drinker.

Her search for someplace to deposit her glass took her into a large darkly paneled room she took to be the living room. The furniture was a disorganized mix of castoffs and secondhand couches. The stereo was precariously perched on a makeshift shelf made from unpainted boards and decorative bricks. She couldn't help but smile at the impression the living room gave her. Obviously, interior decorating held a low priority in the lives of college males.

There were a number of couples in the room, tall muscular men with their arms wrapped around attentive females. Quick calculation told Dawn that this wasn't the place for an odd woman.

She went back the way she'd come, looking desperately for April. But the entryway was empty. This time Dawn followed the sound of female voices into the kitchen, a room that managed to look both littered and neglected at the same time. The kitchen was packed tightly with giggling high-school girls and three or four males who were obviously enjoying all the attention coming their way. None of the males was Brian Riegel.

What was she doing here? she asked herself. She knew most of the girls in the kitchen, but because music was in the air and romance in the night, she couldn't imagine striking up a conversation about a mutual history teacher or whether the new skating rink would open before Christmas.

Dawn had always been influenced by music. It formed her moods. That night the sounds coming from the stereo speakers spoke of taking chances, searching for what had been missing from her life. As the music's spell seeped through her, Dawn made her decision. She could either walk out the front door and wait in the car until April decided to leave, or she could take her courage in hand.

She threw her long hair back over her shoulders, straightened her whisper-white outfit, and began her exploration of the house. April was right. She might never again have the opportunity to get near the man who'd been in her dreams for over a year. It made no sense to feel that way about someone who probably didn't know she was alive, but neither did it make sense to let her life continue to be shaped by hopeless dreams. Brian Riegel, the real Brian Riegel, was there. If she could talk to him, she thought, maybe she would finally see him as a human being and not some creation formed by her dreams. If he was already with someone else, she would slip home and cry her tears, but at least she'd be able to put an end to girlish dreams.

Several of the upstairs bedroom doors were closed. Dawn avoided them. If there were lovers in there, they were entitled to their privacy, she knew. The unoccupied bedrooms continued the same theme of the living room: beds were unmade, clothes were thrown on the floor, and books spilled over desks. In fact, the only objects in the rooms that looked like they'd seen a dust rag were the trophies on dressers or the ribbons tacked to walls. If there was any doubt that this was where some of the college's athletes lived, a glance in the bedrooms quickly dispelled that misconception.

Dawn slipped back downstairs, her thoughts completely taken over by the folk ballad echoing off the walls. It was a song of love, being sung by a woman with a rich, limitless voice. Dawn thought about the faceless singer. Had she ever experienced the kind of love she was singing about? Had she experienced moonlit nights, whispering guitars, and wine?

The smell of cigarette smoke filling the house irritated Dawn's lungs. She sought the front door again, confused and indecisive. She'd received attentive glances from several of the house's residents, but she hadn't returned their bold messages. Dawn felt removed from herself, an echo of the person she thought she was. She moved, dreamlike, to the side of the house and walked slowly toward the large enclosed backyard, where more partygoers were gathered. It was fall. The air held a certain crispness, but because the night was laced with music, Dawn felt only the mood and not the cold. Somehow, she knew, that night would change her.

He was there. Dawn saw him standing under the shelter of an oak tree, engaged in conversation with another man and two girls. He held a beer in his hand, but it looked untouched. If it hadn't been for the music's spell, Dawn would have turned away. It hurt to see him with a girl by his side, but the pain of walking away would be even greater.

Brian Riegel, without shoulder pads and helmet, was no less a man minus the athletic trappings. There was something about his eyes, an attentiveness, that held her motionless. His body was finely tuned, an athlete's physique. He wasn't handsome in a classic sense. His hair should have been cut months ago. His neck was rather thick and his nose slanted slightly to one side, the result, Dawn knew, of having had it broken several years ago. His clothes fit and were clean but looked as if they'd been grabbed off any rack during a flying trip to the nearest clothing store.

Dawn's eyes slid to his hands, hands that could cradle a football as securely as a mother cradles her child. They were so large as to almost be out of proportion to the rest of him.

Dawn wasn't aware of the movement of clouds overhead. They parted briefly, letting free the full moon. The moon erased the dark and sent down a shaft of light to drape itself around Dawn's silvered hair.

Dawn saw the change in Brian's stance, the slow, careful way he turned toward her. The rest of the world faded into the background. At that moment Dawn Morrell and Brian Riegel were the only people in the sheltered yard.

He took a step toward her, then another. Dawn stood trembling. He was coming over to her. He didn't speak. Instead, he stood looking down at her, his chocolate-colored eyes finding their way deep inside her own blue ones. "The moon is glinting off your hair. It's beautiful."

Dawn brought a quick hand to her head. She tried to speak, but his deep voice was rumbling through her, striking her numb.

"Are you with someone?"

Dawn shook her head.

"You're with me now."

Brian didn't touch her. She understood then that he wasn't the kind of man to push himself on a woman and fell even more under his spell because of that. "I know who you are," she said softly.

"But I don't know you." He nodded in the direction of the back porch and then led the way to an ancient and squeaking double seat swing suspended from the porch roof by chains. They sat down together. "What I mean is, I don't know your name," he said in a deep whisper that stirred her senses and warmed her fluttering heart. "I've seen you somewhere, haven't I." It wasn't a question.

Dawn nodded. Their shoulders were touching in the tight confines of the seat. It was as if tentacles of electricity were radiating out from his flesh and bringing her to life. "We went to high school together last year."

"I wonder why I didn't pay more attention to you?"

Dawn smiled. She was alive, truly alive for the first time since she'd become aware of what it meant to be a woman. "I was awfully young," she admitted. "I giggled a lot and ran around in a crowd of girls. I watched you play."

His massive hand found her own small one and gently encompassed it. "I'd say you've grown up a lot from last year. You're not a child."

Had she ever been a child? The feelings stirred by Brian's touch were the feelings of a woman—or at least as close to a woman as she'd ever experienced in her life. Slowly, painfully at first, Dawn told him what it was like to enter high school for the first time, to be aware of the couplings that were taking place among the older students and yet be too young for that herself. "I held hands a few times in the halls last year," she admitted. "I thought I was being terribly mature. Some of my friends had been interested in boys for years, but it took me a while to catch up."

"Holding hands isn't enough anymore, is it?" His eyes slid down her appraisingly. "That isn't the body of a child, Dawn. You're ready to discover what makes men and women different."

"I—I don't know." She trembled under the message in his eyes.

"I do." Slowly, gently, Brian brought his lips to hers. His mouth against hers was like the wings of a butterfly on a sun-warmed cheek. Dawn's senses quivered under the impact of the first time a man's lips had found her heart, the first time she understood the meaning of the word *woman*.

She felt his strong hands on her upper arms as he turned her toward him. Under her soft white sweater Dawn's flesh turned to fire. She was a willing, eager pupil in the hands of a gentle teacher. The next time he sought her lips she was ready, her face turned upward, her eyes closed to capture the moment and hold it to her heart.

"You're an angel. A white angel," Brian whispered under cover of the romantic ballad sung by a woman who knew how to stir the senses. "I'm very glad you came."

That she should be so willing around someone who knew so little about her never entered her mind. All she knew was that she'd been heading toward that moment for a year and whatever happened that night would be part of her for as long as she lived. Brian's fingers were on the exposed silken hairs of her forearms, brushing them so lightly that it was impossible to tell where the night breeze let off and human contact began. Brian brought her sensitive fingers up to his neck and held them firmly against pulsing veins.

Dawn moved closer, not caring, not knowing anything except the moment. She could feel his strong young body through her sweater. In her softly floating state she was no longer certain she wore clothing. She could be naked in this man's arms from the way her flesh was responding.

When again Dawn remembered to breathe, her mind dimly recorded the fact that the woman singer had been replaced by the sweet pure sounds of a single guitar. The sound reached out through the night, drifted upward, and brought down the stars to stand guard over the girl and the man wrapped in each other's arms.

"My God," Brian whispered. "You're beautiful. You're so beautiful."

Dawn's heart sang at the words. Like most girls her age, she'd dreamed of that. But reality was a thousand times better than dreams spun in a lonely bedroom. She wrapped her arms tightly around Brian's neck, clinging to him. Tears born of wonder rose in her throat, making speech impossible. *He's mine! Tonight he's mine!* she thought.

"Dawn? I have to ask you something."

Painfully Dawn brought herself back from the fathomless place she'd been. She opened her eyes and looked into his searching eyes.

"Would you be with me tonight if I wasn't who I am?"

He demanded honesty. Brian Riegel was aware of who he was in the scheme of things in the Rogue Valley. Doubtless he knew that girls were attracted to him because of his deeply masculine image, the mystique that had been woven around him. The athlete who raced down a football field with the hopes of a valley gone football crazy in his arms had no choice but to assume those hopes. Through the media Brian had become the reincarnation of every aging man's youthful dreams, the object of what every matron remembered of innocent days.

"No," she said honestly, and then before he could draw back, she continued. "I—I've been in love with you for a long time. Or maybe I've been infatuated with you all that time. I don't know what the difference is." She laughed. "All I know is, it's a terribly confusing emotion. It was safe. I could dream my dreams without having to face reality. Tonight is reality."

Brian captured her face in capable hands "What's different about tonight?"

Did she dare say what was in her heart? Yes. Yes! This night was too precious for anything but honesty. "I'm no longer dreaming. We're finally together."

"And?"

"And reality is much better."

She'd been praying he'd still want her. Her prayers were answered as his mouth claimed hers. "You're an angel," he whispered before their kiss cut off further words.

Dawn lost herself in the spell of a haunting guitar, the cloaking night, and arms she felt she'd been born to nestle in. They talked, for how long she didn't know. He told her about the difference between high school and college, and she confessed that she couldn't understand why some of her friends felt alienated from their parents, while she continued a close relationship with hers.

When it seemed that they were communicating without words, their conversation took on a new dimension. Gently his hands explored her body in a way that was both sensual and caressing. She'd seen enough of life to realize that love was the goal that sent most men and women on their journey through life, but up until now she had had no concept of the power of that simple word. Dawn's heart, her very being, lay in Brian's capable hands. His fingers and palms ignited feelings she never dreamed existed before. What did she care that others might be watching, that she wasn't the first to feel this man's caresses? Dawn Morrell was coming to life that night. That was all that mattered.

"Let's go inside," he whispered, drawing her to her feet and guiding her to the door. They passed through the noisy kitchen and up the darkened stairs until they could no longer hear voices, only the pure sounds of an instrument fingered lovingly.

Brian took her through the door to his room and closed it behind him. Without asking, he lifted her in his powerful arms and bore her to his bed. She was barely aware of the bed's pressure along her back as he stretched her out and brought her fingers up to his lips. "Don't wake me. If I'm dreaming, I don't want to ever wake up," he whispered. "I've always wanted this."

Don't let it end. Don't ever let it end, Dawn silently told the soft sounds of the guitar spreading out to the corners of the room. Maybe she should hold back. They hadn't touched before tonight. But her heart had known him forever, it seemed.

Slowly, patiently, Brian's fingers taught Dawn everything she needed to know about herself as a woman and her ability to respond sensually. He found the satiny hollow of her throat, the sensitive space inside her elbow, the swell of her breasts. Dawn had no thought of stopping him when he reached behind and unfastened her bra. His lips on her breasts ignited the most exquisite pleasure she'd ever experienced.

Her own fingers became braver, peeling away the barrier of his shirt and buttons and exposing the broad, rock-hard chest covered with nut-colored hair. Brian eased beside her on the bed, bringing them together in an embrace that lasted until Dawn lost all concept of time.

"I want you," he groaned. "But I'll walk out of here if it's not what you want."

Dawn was enough of a woman to know what he was saying. Perhaps she shouldn't have been so willing to give herself to this man who barely knew her, but she was an expert in everything about him. He'd held a special place in her heart for a year. Tonight couldn't be wrong. "I love you," was her answer.

She was going to walk out of the room a woman. Although the realization rocked her and made her body tremble, Dawn knew she'd never look back on it with regret. When a woman was in love, there was only one way of truly expressing that love, Dawn knew.

The music was there, the soft stirring of an instrument overflowing with love ballads. Dawn had given her soul up to that sound, becoming one with it, deepening her conviction that the moment was what she'd been born for. Brian's hands on her flesh were as right as anything had been in her life.

Angel. Had he spoken the word, or was it only an image lingering in the room? It didn't matter. Brian Riegel was with her, loving her, expanding her world in a way that was both ageless and new. She wanted nothing more than to spend the night wrapped in his arms—in his bed.

As his fingers traced the soft line of her hipbones and the hollow between them, Dawn started to tremble. Frightened, she wrapped her arms tightly around him. drawing him to her for security.

"What's wrong?"

"Nothing. I'm a virgin."

Suddenly Brian was no longer there. Dawn's eyes flew open, her arms reaching out for him. He was leaning over her, his warm breath striking her on the cheek. In the dark she could barely read the message flashing in his dun-colored eyes. "A virgin?"

"Brian? Please. Don't look at me that way. It's all right." She could barely speak with him staring at her like that.

But instead of surrendering to her outstretched arms, Brian moaned and surged away. He stood poised and tense, his face twisted in pain. "I didn't know."

"What—what did you think?"

Angrily he shook his head. "I didn't think. That's the hell of it. I'm sorry, angel. God, I'm sorry."

"Why?" Her arms still reached for him but he denied her his strength as he put on his clothes. "Please. What's wrong?"

"Child. You're a child."

He was gone, the door slamming behind him, hollow music the only thing he'd left behind. Dawn sobbed her heartbreak into the empty room and wrapped her lonely arms around her trembling body. He didn't want her! Brian Riegel didn't want her! She'd been pulled from the game without having had a time at bat. No one told her the rules would allow that.

Dawn pushed herself out of bed and went to stare out the window at the stars. There was no guitar tonight, no girl-woman crying in pain and confusion.

But she still remembered the agony from all those years ago. It had eventually been buried in the act of living, going to college, working, a motorcycle accident... but it was still there.

Damn you, Brian Riegel! You had no right making me fall in love with you! Why is it so hard getting over you? Ten years should be enough time! Some day she was going to bury her nails in his flesh and demand an answer. If that night had been a game played by an arrogant, self-confident male, then he was much crueler than anyone she'd ever met. Didn't he know how vulnerable, how helpless she'd been that night? Dawn asked herself. Bringing her to the brink of womanhood, of ecstasy, and then slamming a door between them had been the most brutal thing anyone had ever done to her.

As the stars erased the cobwebs of night Dawn stared at her shaken reflection and forced herself to face reality. She was still terribly vulnerable around Brian Riegel. Insulating herself from further pain was going to take all the vigilance she was capable of. But she was determined. The game of love carried more risks than baseball ever could.

Chapter Five

Anticipation raced down Dawn's spine. She felt an excitement she hadn't known since her first day of work at Cook County Hospital. No matter that she'd spent the night caught in the web of the past. This morning marked a new inning in her life, the reason behind months spent studying sports medicine. True, Brian was bound to be there when the newly signed players filed onto Verdue Field, but she was determined to keep a blanket over her emotions and concentrate on what she was being paid for.

It wasn't yet 9:00 A.M. when she pulled her little car beside the Verdue Field van and stepped out. From head to toe she mirrored the all-American image of the female athlete. Her feet fit comfortably in a new pair of running shoes. Her cream sweat pants and matching pullover sports top were accented with a vertical strip of lavender that ran from neck to sleeve and was picked up again in the twin strips tracing a line down her hips. She'd caught her hair back in a loose tie at the base of her neck. Except for a touch of lipstick that doubled as lip moisturizer, she wore no makeup.

The sight of the van unnerved her slightly, but she squared her shoulders and stepped through the side entrance marked Employees Only.

She was slightly nonplussed to find that Ralph Mercer was already there and setting up his photography equipment. But this morning he barely glanced her way. The reason for his attention to business immediately became evident. Already a half dozen well-muscled young men were throwing to each other in the infield. According to what Brian had told her, the ink on their contracts was barely dry following the annual baseball draft. Since most of them were coming from out of state, she hadn't expected them to be out of their motel rooms and attending to business so early.

But after watching the players warming up for several minutes, she knew why they were here. The eagerness they felt for the direction their lives were taking was evident in their hustle, in the way their voices echoed off the stands. And why not? These young men had dreamed of becoming professional ballplayers since childhood. Today—at Verdue Field—the first part of that dream was coming true.

"They're an eager lot," Dawn heard someone say, and turned to see a man carrying a TV camera setup walking over to Ralph. Although Dawn hadn't been in town long enough to recognize any of the local TV newscasters, the TV station's logo was stamped on the camera's side. The arrival of professional ballplayers had obviously attracted countywide attention.

"You got a list of their names?" Ralph was asking the paunchy, balding man weighed down under the weight of his equipment. "I messed up on that."

"Damn. I left it in my car. Wouldn't you know it? Now I'll have to go back." Disgust was in the man's voice.

Dawn stepped toward them. No matter what her feelings for Ralph, she was a member of the A's organization. It wouldn't be right not to share what information she had with the news media. She pulled the list she'd gotten from Brian out of her pocket and handed it to Ralph. "Can you copy off the names and statistics and give it back to me? I don't want to start talking to them without knowing their names."

Ralph gave her a wide-eyed look and accepted the offered sheets. "What was your opinion of the article? Think it'll help bring people to the games?"

"You did a good job," she admitted. "Thank you."

A decided leer changed Ralph's expression. "I can think of a more sincere way of thanking me."

"Lay off the poor kid," the TV man interrupted. "Ralph, you'd make a pass at a drugstore Indian if it was wearing a skirt. I'm sorry." He turned toward Dawn. "Not that you look like a drugstore Indian. Far from it. I've got to get a shot of you before this is over."

"Oh, don't," Dawn protested. "The ballplayers are the story. Not me."

"You let me be the judge of that, young lady," the TV man said, patting her paternally on the shoulder.

"Is there any chance of getting you to attend to business?" Brian's harsh question cut through the cool morning air.

Dawn whirled. She hadn't done anything wrong. What could he possibly object to? A sharp retort was on her lips, but it died. Standing at Brian's side, his little hand caught in Brian's big one, was a boy Dawn took to be five or six years old. His auburn hair caught the morning sunlight, which also pointed up the freckles on his little nose. If Dawn hadn't looked into the little boy's eyes, she wouldn't have taken him for who he was. But the open nut-brown eyes staring up at her were mirrors of Verdue Field's general manager.

All thoughts of Brian were pushed aside as she bent forward and winked at the little boy. "Are you one of the players?" she asked. "You look kind of young, but if you have a strong throwing arm, that's all that matters."

The boy looked up at his father for reassurance and then smiled tentatively. "I can throw way out there." He pointed toward center field.

"I bet you can." Dawn warmed to the boy instantly. He was clinging to his father's hand in the way of a small child thrust into the company of adults, but he wasn't afraid to talk. "What position do you play?" she asked seriously.

"I'm a pitcher."

Dawn grinned at the boy's self-confident response. "You know, I heard something. I'm not sure I believe it. Someone told me that pitchers aren't very good hitters. What do you think?"

"I have a bat. It has Steve Garvey's name on it."

"Well, if you can hit as good as Steve Garvey, I'm glad you're going to be on the team. A pitcher, did you say? We certainly can use someone who can mix up his curves and sliders."

All the time the lighthearted exchange was going on, Dawn was aware of Brian's eyes on her. They glowed with a light she couldn't fathom, but the impact was such that if it hadn't been for a tremendous effort, she would have faltered. She couldn't decide whether he approved of her speaking to his son or not. "The rest of the players will be here in a few minutes," he observed. "Don't you think you should get out there where you can get a good look at them?"

"Thank you, sir! I appreciate the advice," Dawn said through jaws tight with tension. "But I think I can handle my job without your help."

"That remains to be seen," Brian shot back and turned on his heels.

Dawn retrieved her player list from a grinning Ralph and stared in confusion at Brian's back. If he wasn't the most unsettling man she'd ever met! "What's his boy's name?" she asked.

Ralph only shrugged. "Beats me. I didn't even know he was married. Most closemouthed man I've ever seen. I wonder where his wife is. He's going to be out here all day, and the kid's going to get tired. What we don't need is some whining kid."

Was Brian married? she wondered. Nothing he'd said had given any hint of a wife. Dawn tried to tell herself that the answer wasn't important. Surely she was no longer the love-struck schoolgirl who had surfaced briefly last night. Brian had gone on to live his own life just as she'd carved out a career for herself. There was no longer anything between them—if in fact there had ever been.

He was obviously very content in his role as a father. The way he walked with his head bent toward his chattering son told her that being with his child was a pleasure and not a baby-sitting chore.

Reluctantly Dawn followed after Brian until she found herself standing along the foul line, watching the players warming up. The team manager, a thin little man built with what looked like coiled wire for muscles, had joined Brian, and the two were watching the proceedings intently. Dawn had met the fiftyish man who insisted on being called Coach Weatherby yesterday and was impressed by his seemingly limitless knowledge of baseball, despite a disheveled appearance and a frame that looked too ancient for the task he had taken on. As he explained, he'd been involved with baseball for so many years that he wore the title coach in the same way that most men placed Mr. in front of their names.

Dawn was concentrating on the activities on the field when she felt something soft pressing against her elbow. When she looked down, Brian's son was standing facing her. "I didn't bring my bat today," he said. "Do you want to see it?"

"You better believe I do." If Brian didn't like her talking to his son, that was too bad, Dawn decided. The youngster was too much of a charmer to ignore. "What do you think of those men out there? Think we can whip them into a ball club?"

"They're big. When I grow up, I'm going to play for the Astros. They have the best uniforms."

There was no arguing with that conviction, Dawn thought. "You sound like you've watched a lot of baseball," she observed.

"With my dad." The words were said proudly. "Mom doesn't like baseball. She turns it off when it comes on TV."

"Oh." Did the little boy have any idea how much

his simple sentence had revealed? Probably not. Children were direct simply because they saw no reason to be otherwise.

"Tad, don't bother the lady."

"He's not bothering me," she told Brian. "He's a lot more interesting to talk to than certain adults." Tad? The name fit the animated child.

"And a lot more interesting than doing your job. I don't suppose you have a little speech worked out, do you? I want you to address the players this morning."

"Thank you, sir." She saluted smartly to give her hand something to do. "I'm sorry to disappoint you, but I do know what I want to tell them. You didn't inform me that you wanted a formal meeting, but I'll do my best to carry it off." She didn't like speaking critically around Tad's father, but since the man obviously couldn't manage to be civil around her, she didn't seem to have a choice.

"That's a relief" was all he said to her. "Tad, I think we're going to need some more balls. Why don't you run over to the equipment room and get them."

Tad's eyes glowed at the responsibility he was being given. He broke away from Dawn and ran on short, pumping legs in the direction his father had pointed.

Dawn tore her eyes from the boy, catching the expression on Brian's face as she did so. Gone was the attentive, intense look of a businessman, the critical glare when he stared at her. Instead, a soft light radiated out from his eyes and encompassed his whole being. Brian's mouth softened into a proud grin as he watched his son hurrying on his mission.

Whatever else Brian Riegel was, he was a deeply loving father.

"He doesn't look much like you, except in the eyes," she observed. "And his hands. He's going to have big hands."

"Big feet too." Brian's attention was still on the child. "I bought him a pair of shoes last month, and he's already filled them out." Brian turned toward Dawn. At that instant she saw a curtain drop over his expression, erasing the glow his son had put there. "I'm sure you're not interested in that. Unfortunately, his mother has a tendency to overlook such things as too-small shoes. Someone has to attend to such details."

"His mother." Not "my wife." Was there significance in that? she wondered. Dawn had little opportunity to dwell on that question, since as soon as Tad delivered the bulging ball bag, Coach Weatherby called the players together and started explaining that today's practice was informal but designed to give him some indication of each player's ability. Dawn knew enough about what was going on in the young men's minds to realize they'd all be competing for the manager's attention. It meant she'd be given the opportunity to assess each player's capabilities and limitations from a trainer's standpoint. Already sweat was glistening on their faces, proof that they weren't holding back.

While Coach Weatherby directed the morning workout from his position near the batter's box, and Ralph and the TV man stationed themselves just outside the wire fencing, Dawn leaned forward against the low fencing separating the dugout from the playing fields.

She put on sunglasses and was able to concentrate on individual players without their being aware and perhaps self-conscious.

Brian had gone off to answer the phone ringing in his office, but Tad stayed behind, slowly inching himself closer until his nose was pressed against the wire, his never-still elbow tickling Dawn's side. After a minute of comfortable silence, Dawn tapped the boy on the shoulder to get his attention. "Aren't you supposed to be in school?" she asked. "Summer vacation hasn't started yet, has it?"

Tad shook his head. "Dad came and got me today, 'cause he thought I'd rather be here. We were just going to draw in school anyway. I don't like drawing."

"What do you like? Lunch?"

Tad grinned up at her, letting her know she'd hit the nail on the head. "And recess."

"Ah, yes," Dawn mused. "Recess was always my favorite time too. It was best when we got a baseball game going and the boys let the girls play. Do you like reading?"

"We don't read in kindergarten. Just counting. I know all my colors."

"Oh." Dawn suppressed a grin. Obviously, Tad thought her not quite bright for not being aware of certain basic facts. "Well, do you think you're going to like reading?"

Tad nodded. "Then I can read the sports page."

"You sound like your dad. You both like sports, don't you?"

"Mom doesn't. She says it's dumb."

Dawn couldn't think of a response. It was clear to her that Tad was in the dark about his mother's opinion of sports. But she wasn't going to question Tad's mother's likes and dislikes in front of her son. Tad seemed content to watch the infielders running down grounders, and Dawn concentrated too, making mental notes about which foot different players used to lead off with and watching for any sign of slowness in arm muscle strength.

Brian rejoined them, silent and concentrating on the action on the field. His arm went easily around Tad's shoulders, drawing the boy toward him. Once he dipped his body to plant a kiss on the auburn head. Dawn found herself wishing it were she who held the small boy. Hospital work had brought her in contact with many youngsters. It always left her sad to have the children turn to their parents and not to her for comfort. Her consolation had been to tell herself that her time for mothering would come.

Her response to having Brian standing nearby was more confusing. Her body was being drawn toward his, a moth heading toward the light. A fathomless warmth was spreading through her, making her both alarmed and contented in a way she wondered if she'd ever been before. If he'd put an arm around her, she would have leaned toward him, fulfilled.

He was a man. Of that she was acutely aware. But why should she be so deeply affected by that? It wasn't as if she'd never had a date since that magic night ten years ago. Her relationship with Jim before the accident had advanced to the point of them talking in terms of a future together. But romance hadn't been part of their relationship during Jim's months of physical therapy, and when she told him she was taking a new job and moving, he hadn't tried to stop her.

Was she reacting to Brian's nearness simply because she wasn't involved with a man and hadn't been, in a romantic way, for a long time? She wasn't sure she was up to admitting that beneath her calm exterior beat the heart of a passionate woman aching for physical intimacy. It wasn't like her to be attracted to a man simply in a physical way. And yet she didn't really know enough about who Brian was these days to be reacting to him in any other context—just as she hadn't really known him when she'd been so willing to share his bed.

"You're not taking notes," Brian observed. "Don't tell me you have a photographic memory?"

If she hadn't been struggling so against her reaction to being near Brian, Dawn would have remembered that a five-year-old boy was privy to their conversation. But her reaction to his obvious criticism set her off. "You amaze me, Mr. Riegel. With everything you have to attend to, I don't understand why you are so interested in something as trivial as whether I'm taking notes or not."

"I'm simply trying to ascertain whether the organization made the best choice in choosing you for this job."

Dawn bit her tongue against a biting retort and struggled for composure. "I'm not the same child I was the last time we were, uh, thrown together. I've grown up."

"I'm sorry to hear that. I believe we'd all be better off if we retained some childlike qualities." His face darkened. "We lose too much of our ability to enjoy life when we grow up."

"Is growing up all that bad?" she asked, momen

tarily heartened because he no longer seemed to be finding fault with her. "At least the big boys don't kick sand in my face and tell me a brat girl can't play football. I can't say the years since I turned twenty-one have been all bad."

"You didn't get married."

Dawn glanced quickly at Tad to see if the boy was listening. Fortunately, he appeared to be wrapped up in watching the high, strong arc of a fly ball heading toward center field. "Marriage is supposed to be a goal, not a punishment," she observed.

"It all depends on how you've been affected by it. Forget it." Brian jammed his hands against the wire railing. "I'm not going to ruin today by going over that tired old subject. It's just that thanks to a couple of lawyers bent on dragging things out, I haven't been allowed to think of much else lately."

Dawn turned back to the action on the field. She could almost feel the weight of the curtain Brian had just drawn around himself. The man standing beside her was no longer the young athlete she'd given her heart to. This man had dark moods and memories, emotions she felt were coloring his relationship with her. Wasn't it bad enough that she hadn't mastered the art of laying aside her teen years and forgetting that once he'd been the most important person in her life? Why did their relationship have to be complicated by emotions of his own? she wanted to know.

Tad was the lucky one. His life stretched before him like a smooth wide ocean. He was unaware of storms and treacherous undercurrents. "What would you do if someone hit a foul ball at us?" she asked the boy in an attempt to lighten the air around them. "Do you think you could duck fast enough?"

"I don't have to duck. I have a glove. I can catch anything with this." He held up a catcher's mitt so large, he had to hold it with both hands.

Brian shook his head. "I thought I asked you to get baseballs, young man. I didn't say anything about a mitt. Besides, where's yours? You didn't lose the one I gave you, did you?"

"Mom said I wouldn't need it. She made me leave it on my bed so I wouldn't lose it."

Again Brian's fingers tightened on the fencing. He said nothing, but the taut line of his jaw spoke volumes. Dawn longed to reach out and smooth away the pressure there, but she knew better than to touch him. The last thing Brian Riegel would want from her was a show of sympathy.

The silence that existed between them was enough to drive Dawn to distraction. She'd always enjoyed being in the company of someone who didn't find it necessary to fill the air with senseless chatter, but this silence was tight, not soothing. It seemed clear to Dawn that Brian regretted every moment he had to spend in her presence. Otherwise he wouldn't be so critical of her. Given the freedom to do so, she would have turned and walked away from Verdue Field.

But she couldn't. Like Brian, she had a job here.

When Coach Weatherby at last called a halt to the workout, Dawn felt as if she'd been given a reprieve. Now, finally, she had something to do. She walked out onto the field where the young players were standing around the manager and waited until he was through speaking.

Only when she was sure she had their attention did she explain why she was here. As she expected, the announcement that she was the team's trainer and charged with their physical conditioning was met with wolf calls and winks. "I'm afraid you're going to be mistaken." She laughed. "I was graduated from high school when most of you were still learning your multiplication tables. That makes me an old woman."

"If you're an old woman, I want my cradle robbed."

Dawn ignored the remark. She'd expected it to take a while to gain their respect. She was ready to begin the process. "When I was in school, I saw a lot of people, both boys and girls, who made up the most elaborate excuses to avoid taking phys ed. I expect exactly the opposite was the case with all of you." She waited to be sure they were looking at her before continuing. "If anything, I'm going to see the unfortunate results of overtraining more than undertraining. You're all reaching for the brass ring. You're going to keep on pushing yourselves until your bodies rebel against you."

"I'll put my body in your hands. Please! Let me put your body in my hands."

Dawn faced her teaser. The barrel-chested man probably stood six feet four with a hardness around his mouth that made him look older than she knew he had to be. "What's your name?"

"Bob Webber. The girls call me Big Bob." He took a step toward her, his whole demeanor taunting.

"I'll call you Robert. Listen to me, Robert, I seriously doubt that you talked to your teachers the way you're talking to me. I'm not going to stand for it any more than they would have. If you can't keep a civil tongue in your mouth, then maybe you don't belong here.''

Bob Webber was momentarily silenced, but Dawn sensed he wasn't done with her yet. Nonetheless, she turned back to the others, determined to keep the situation under control. ''I want each of you to report to me every time you experience pain,'' she continued. ''Pain is the warning signal your body puts out when it's under stress. If you feel discomfort in your muscles, bones, or joints, don't ignore it. I know you're probably thinking that I'll have you sitting on the bench if you tell me about a physical problem. Maybe I will. That has to be decided on an individual basis.''

''I'm going to tough it out,'' Big Bob declared. ''A player who sits on the bench doesn't move up in the system.''

''That's not necessarily true,'' Dawn countered. She wished it wasn't Bob who had brought up that point, but it had to be dealt with. ''If you ignore an injury and keep putting that joint or muscle or whatever under stress, it's only going to get worse. You can either sit on the bench for a day or two and get proper treatment, or you can run the risk of winding up in the hospital.'' She turned to the other players. ''The decision is yours. Either trust me to know what to do for an injury, or play Russian roulette with your future as ballplayers.''

Apparently, Dawn's remark had the desired response. Dawn had the full attention of the men as she went over her conditioning program, which included a regular routine of running, in addition to the standard exercises and weight lifting. The men acknowledged that they engaged in regular stretching warm-ups before a game, but few of them understood the reason for stretching out muscles. Briefly she explained that hard exercise shortens muscles and makes them more susceptible to pulls and strains. "Treat your body like a machine and it'll respond like one," she finished up. "One more point. I will not tolerate the use of drugs by anyone. If you're injured, we'll do what has to be done to heal that injury. I'm not going to give you a painkiller and send you out on the field. If you're in real pain, you need a doctor, not me. As far as I'm concerned, amphetamines—uppers—do more harm than good. Anyone who uses drugs has no business in professional athletics."

Even as Brian took over to discuss the players' living arrangements Dawn continued to feel pumped up. She'd rehearsed the points she wanted to make enough times that she felt she'd accomplished what she'd set out to do. Bob Webber had continued to stare at her with challenging eyes, but he was a minority.

Maybe it was Verdue Field, Dawn thought as she became aware of how warm the day was. Probably most of these young ballplayers never had the opportunity to play on a professionally maintained diamond. Today their dreams were one step closer to becoming reality. Dawn was part of that dream, and as such part of the professional baseball franchise they now had contracts with. No matter what her sex, she was as much a part of the system as the manager or the general manager.

It was easy to put herself in their shoes. Hadn't she spun her daydreams around a young man in shoulder pads and a football helmet? These young men had their own dreams.

Hopefully, for a few of them at least, dreams would become reality.

And for the rest of them? They would have to face facts just as she had. The real world was sometimes quite different from the spells spun in an innocent teenager's head. A football hero becomes a man with a son and business concerns. A girl lays aside idealistic dreams of a fairy-tale romance and settles for something else.

But it complicates things when the object of her dreams comes back into her life. Dawn watched Brian as he talked, his now-weary son hanging on to him. He was the kind of man a child would turn to, and that made him even more dangerous. Every time Dawn looked at Brian, she was reminded of her complete surrender in his arms that night so long ago. Was he still capable of controlling her in that way?

That was what she was determined to guard against. Brian was tied to Tad's mother. Maybe they weren't married—the hints he'd dropped led her to believe that—but the child she'd borne was an integral part of Brian's life, and thus mother and father could never go their separate ways. Besides, Brian's behavior toward Dawn made it clear that he was determined to keep her at arm's length.

"I want nothing to do with you, not on a personal basis," was the message in his eyes.

Fine. It was the message her now-wiser heart was giving her. No one wants to spend the whole game sitting on the bench.

Finally, Brian released the players. They had been

told that they'd be staying at an older hotel unless they preferred other accommodations. "I'd suggest you look into renting apartments or houses. The price of the hotel is right, but I've seen enough of it to know that you're not going to feel as if you're part of the community if you stay there. Be here tomorrow at nine," Brian said, and scooped his son up in his arms.

Dawn was detained by a bean pole of a first baseman who asked advice on how to add pounds to his frame. By the time she was done talking to him, Verdue Field was nearly devoid of ballplayers, and the TV man was packing away his equipment. Ralph had already left.

Dawn felt reluctant to leave. It was barely noon, and yet her day's work was done. The heat was enough to make her want to change into shorts and pull off her running shoes, but that didn't seem appropriate. Suddenly an idea struck her. If Tad was still around, maybe he'd want to go somewhere for an ice-cream cone.

She could hear childish giggling coming from Brian's office and walked through the open door. Brian had draped a numbered shirt over his son's shoulders. The uniform was dragging on the ground, much to Tad's delight.

"I think the laundry sent the wrong size," Dawn observed. "Either that or you've shrunk. I understand that ice cream is good for growing boys. Would you like to join me in a treat?"

Tad's face lit up, but it was overshadowed by the dark glare radiating from his father. "I have to get him home," Brian said. "It's in the custody agreement. I would think you'd have the sense to check things out with me before making such a tempting offer."

One look at Tad's crushed expression and Dawn knew she couldn't allow Brian's angry words to stand unchallenged. "I'm sorry if I interfered with your arrangement with your son and your ex-wife," she offered diplomatically. "But I assure you, the offer was made in good faith. It doesn't take that long to eat an ice-cream cone."

Dawn could sense the tension in Brian's body as he stood looming over her. For a moment she wondered if he had enough self-control to keep from seizing her. The force of his considerable masculinity held her riveted, incapable of planning how she would act in her defense. His reaction made no sense. What had she done to enrage him?

Suddenly he reached out and grabbed her arms, yanking her roughly closer. They stood, bodies touching, as he stared down at her, his viselike hands sending electrical charges coursing through her taut nerve endings. She should be thinking of defense, she realized, but the affect of being in his arms effectively stripped her of all thought other than being overwhelmingly aware of his maleness.

"Brian? What—"

"You want an ice-cream cone! All right. Who am I to dash cold water on your pleasure." Still gripping her tightly, Brian started to propel Dawn toward the exit, an obviously confused Tad in tow. Dawn submitted, stumbling and being forced to reach for Brian to steady herself. His physical presence enveloped her and left her unable to think of anything save what he'd done to her usually dependable emotions. She was barely aware of where they were going as he yanked open the door to the van and shoved her inside. A moment later he'd lifted Tad into the van's rear cavern and was starting the engine.

Dawn sat trembling and uncertain as his sure hands gripped the wheel and his raging expression masked the gentle light that claimed his eyes when he was with his son earlier.

Despite herself, she was being drawn to Brian. No longer was he an untested youth. He had become a man capable of emotions she couldn't understand, anger that made her tremble. But the man he'd become was nevertheless of deep interest to her. What Brian was today was reality. The youth a girl could spin her dreams around had given way to that.

And yet the way Brian conducted himself made her all too aware of the chances she was taking around him. "I hope you're not in the habit of losing your temper all the time," she offered. "You're going to frighten your son if you do that."

"What do you know about self-control?" Brian asked through molded lips. "Unless you've tangled with your wife—ex-wife—for your child, you don't know anything about maintaining self-control."

Brian's terse statement stopped her. The bitterness laced through his words spoke more than the words themselves. *Hot and cold* described the man perfectly. Hot in his devotion to his son, cold in his attitude toward the mother of that son. Why his anger should be directed toward her as well was a mystery, but now was not the time to demand an answer.

Instead, she shifted around in the high sturdy bucket seat so she could carry on a conversation with

Tad. As they spoke of baseball and bicycles she tried not to think about how close her legs were to Brian's thighs, but there was no denying that being in close proximity with the man did things to her senses that she had scant control over.

She set her muscles as the van slowed, but she didn't turn around until Brian had cut the engine. They were parked in front of an ice-cream parlor that proclaimed its large variety of flavors on a sign flanked by flashing red lights. The effect was, in Dawn's mind, garish, but obviously Tad was delighted. He crawled between the bucket seats and was scrambling out over his father's lap almost before Brian was ready for the wriggling burden.

Dawn was left to make her way into the parlor alone. As she joined Brian and Tad at the counter she reached for her purse because, after all, the treat had been her idea, but an icy stare from Brian stopped her. Obviously, he wasn't about to let her buy what turned out to be Tad's double-decker chocolate-strawberry combination. Dawn selected a single scoop of mint herself and held her tongue as Brian paid for all three of them.

Tad climbed up on the spindly wire chair and leaned forward on the round table, intent on the chore of finishing his cone before it could start to drip. Brian ate in silence, his bulk seeming too much for the fragile piece of furniture.

Slowly, to Dawn's great relief, Brian began to relax. He asked his son a few questions about his reaction to a morning spent at Verdue Field and laughed in delight at the child's response. Soon Dawn entered the conversation with observations of her own. For a few minutes the barriers were stripped away. Casual observers would have taken the three for a loving couple on an outing with their son.

"So you think you'll be able to play with those guys in a few years," Brian teased his son gently. "What do you think you'll have to do to make the team?"

"Exercise," Tad answered confidently. "And lift weights. Like Dawn says."

"And you think Dawn's an expert?"

Tad nodded vigorously. Obviously, he had no reservations about Dawn's expertise.

"We'll just have to wait and see if the players share your opinion," Brian said without looking at Dawn.

For her part Dawn refused to be sucked into Brian's offhanded challenge. She was enjoying the moment too much to let it be ruined by anything Brian might say. Through her work at the hospital she often developed relationships with children. But the children she attended to were frightened and apprehensive. It was a rare treat to be able to be in the company of a happy child. If Brian hadn't been there, she would have pressed Tad to her, soaking in the open honesty of the boy. It made her ache for the day when she would have a son or a daughter of her own. Whatever her mother might think about Dawn's devotion to a career, Dawn was still an old-fashioned woman.

Of course, having a baby would require a man, and so far Dawn had been unable to find one she was ready to raise her children with. Her early crush on Brian had been colored with such concentrated emotional intensity that the thought of an everyday existence never occurred to her. The teenage Dawn thought no further than moonlit nights and mornings waking up in Brian's arms.

That was a thousand dreams ago. Dawn was now mature enough to realize that evening sunsets invariably gave way to alarms ringing in the morning.

"Are you ready to leave? I'm not in a position to challenge the custody arrangement, at least not yet. I have to get Tad home."

Dawn tried to avoid the tight expression on Brian's face as he leaned over to wipe Tad's chin, but there was no misreading his words. Whatever agreement existed between Brian and his ex-wife as far as Tad was concerned didn't sit well with Brian. Dawn was still watching the emotions playing in Brian's eyes as he stood up. For a moment Brian's face froze and then it was there—an instant of physical pain!

Dawn's eyes flashed to Brian's hands. He was gripping the table with white knuckles, the veins standing out in vivid contrast to tanned flesh. Dawn knew she'd perceived the reason when she saw how long it took him to put his weight on his right leg.

"What's wrong?" she asked, reaching out to lend a hand.

Brian pulled away. "Nothing for you to concern yourself with," he said. "I'll be contacting a doctor, thank you."

Upset because he'd put her off so roughly, Dawn quickly took her seat in the van when they were outside. With an effort she threw off her mood and concentrated on the passing landscape. They were heading toward where Tad lived with his mother, and Dawn wanted to have some impression of the neighborhood.

The modern apartment complex surprised her. The Tower Arms was expertly landscaped and maintained, complete with swimming pool and sauna and wooden siding on the building instead of the formless stucco common to so many apartments, but, somehow, it wasn't right.

As she sat waiting for Brian to return from delivering Tad she decided what it was. This wasn't a place for a boy like Tad to grow up. Where were the lawns for a child to run and roll on? Where was a dirt hill for bike riding? To the side of Tower Arms was a four-lane road; on the other was the back of a small exclusive shopping center.

Children needed fields, creeks, and hills, and trees to climb. None of the simple pleasures of childhood was available for the youngsters living at Tower Arms. She couldn't see much of the crowded playground, but she knew that the two swings and single slide wouldn't long entertain an active boy. No wonder he'd been delighted to have Verdue Field to roam in.

When he returned, Brian didn't attempt to break the silence. For a moment he sat leaning against the wheel, his hooded eyes on the tastefully decorated building. Dawn sensed rather than heard his muttered oath as he pumped the van into life. She stole a glance at him and wasn't surprised to see the hard line of his jaw.

"Were you late?" she ventured. "I hope I didn't cause any problems."

"Don't worry. The problems have been there for a long time. You didn't add to them." He allowed himself a small smile. "Lori's going to be out of town next week. Business trip, she calls it. She wants me to keep Tad."

"You're going to be busy—"

"I'm never too busy for my son. If I had him—

Never mind. I'm not going to get ahead of myself. I suppose you want to be taken back to your car?''

"If that's not too much trouble."

"It doesn't matter." His jaw worked for a moment and then just as quickly as his dark mood had descended, Brian switched gears and started an impersonal conversation about the season's prospects. As the van retraced its route to Verdue Field, Brian concentrated on working out a schedule for the team that would make for maximum training and practice while still allowing the young men the freedom to become comfortable in their new surroundings. "I remember how much energy kids that age have. Two of them are married. The others are going to be interested in finding girl friends, taking in the local night spots. Unfortunately, at that age hormones get in the way of a man's commitment to his career. It isn't going to be easy to strike the right balance."

Dawn agreed. She pointed out that physical activity provided an excellent outlet for excess energy, but she had no delusions that baseball was all the players had on their minds. It felt good to be talking to Brian on a professional level. For the first time she wondered if maybe he did respect her capabilities, after all. At least he wasn't making any cutting remarks.

All too soon they were back at the Verdue Field parking lot, now deserted except for Dawn's little car. She let herself out, aware despite herself that Brian was slow in getting out and moving around to her side of the van. He'd been out working with the players part of the morning. Dawn couldn't help worry that the physical exertion had taken its toll on a knee that had already been subjected to too much punishment in the past. The tight lines at the corners of Brian's mouth were the only indication that her assessment of the situation was right.

She started toward her car, but Brian stopped her by placing a restraining hand around her upper right arm. Slowly he turned her around and stared down at her. Instinctively Dawn lifted her head, her mouth. A dry wind chased itself in the parking lot, whipping up little bits of dust, but except for that unheeded intrusion the only sound Dawn was aware of was the primitive beating of her heart.

Past, present, the future, even, held nothing for her. She existed only for this moment with Brian Riegel standing next to her. She whimpered deep in her throat as he pulled her against him and wrapped his powerful arms around her back, making her his willing captive.

His kiss was all her feminine instincts had hoped for. He bore down on her, both gentle and passionate. Her eyes closed to better block out the world, and she parted her lips to receive his unspoken message.

She felt unhinged from head to foot, a formless emotion floating in a swell of feeling beyond her capacity to perceive. Ten years ago Brian Riegel had taken a girl in his arms and given her a taste of womanhood. Today, in an empty parking lot with the high walls of Verdue Field to shelter them, he gave her another taste of that womanhood.

And then, just as suddenly, he thrust her from him.

Chapter Six

Crystal Morrell was setting out a plate of cheese and crackers on the redwood table that sat to one side of her back patio. Dawn watched her mother appraisingly. There'd been a time when she wondered if her mother would survive intact after her husband's death. But obviously Crystal had more emotional fortitude than her daughter had been aware of.

"Are you sure you can't stay, dear?" Crystal was saying. "I'm delighted you can meet Peter, but I wish you'd stay and eat with us."

Dawn shook her head. "I'm going to give myself a nervous breakdown if I don't get settled in. I can't believe I've been here for almost three weeks and there are still boxes sitting in the spare room."

"I'm just pleased to hear you're enjoying your job so much. I know you haven't been working with the ballplayers very long, but what do you think of them? What kind of relationship do you think you'll have with them? Are they going to take your advice?"

"They better." Dawn folded napkins and placed silverware on them to keep the wind from blowing them away. "After all, I'm an old lady and they're a bunch of kids."

"I don't know why you insist on putting it like that. You can't be more than five or six years older than those kids."

"Next to them I feel a hundred years old." Dawn dropped her eyes, aware of the silent message lurking in them. "They're so optimistic about life. They haven't seen much of its hard knocks."

"And you have? I know that accident and everything you went through with Jim was a sobering experience, but I can't believe I've lost my upbeat girl." Crystal patted her daughter's head. "If I remember correctly, you were the unstoppable dreamer. Do you remember when you declared yourself to be in love with that movie actor? How many letters did you send him?"

"None. I tore them up—fortunately. I did go off the deep end a bit in those days, didn't I? I can't believe I was such a romantic." Or could she? The crush on the movie actor had lasted less than a month. What she felt for Brian had endured for longer than she cared to admit. The fact was, she wasn't sure it had ever died. A moment in his arms three days ago had reawakened emotions she'd thought had been buried ten years ago. The fact that she'd barely seen him since he'd spun out of the parking lot had done little to help realign her life.

"Romance is what makes the world go around," Crystal was saying. "Oh, I know it's an old-fashioned opinion these days. Women are supposed to be independent and concentrating on careers and fulfilling themselves and all that. But"—Crystal's voice became reflective—"without someone to share that life with, it doesn't have much meaning."

"Mom?" Dawn placed her arms around her mother's shoulders. "I don't know if you want to talk about it, but I can't help but worry about you. Are you really all right these days?"

"Do you mean have I gotten over your father's death?" Crystal shook her head. "I don't think that will ever happen. I don't want it to. Honey, we shared something special. That won't change. I hope someday you'll see what I mean. Someday you're going to fall in love, really in love. No matter what happens in your life from then on, that love will remain an island, a part of your heart you hold separate. It's like finding that exquisite jewel and being able to appreciate it for all it stands for." Crystal laughed. "Listen to me. I never thought of myself as a philosopher, but I mean what I'm saying. Love turns on all the lights in a woman. At least it did for me. When your father was alive, I believed that love would come only once for me. I was happy with that. But—I like the way I feel when I'm with Peter now."

It didn't take Dawn long to understand why her mother felt the way she did. Peter arrived ten minutes later. He was only a few inches taller than her mother and his body showed the effects of having spent his working life behind a desk, but when he shook hands with her, his grip was firm and his eyes met hers without wavering. He didn't push himself on her; Dawn appreciated that. Instead, he began a spirited conversation about one of his pet projects—maintaining open space in the county that could be used for youth activities.

By the time Dawn had hauled herself back to her

house to finish the long-neglected chore of moving in, she was in favor of her mother's choice. Peter was a man she could develop a lasting friendship with. No wonder Crystal had said what she had. *"Love turns on all the lights in a woman."* What a beautiful way her mother had phrased it.

Dawn didn't want to think about the lights that had burst into being simply because Brian had kissed her, but as she went about the chore of arranging books on the living room bookshelf, her mind returned to that all-too-brief moment. Why had he kissed her? And why had he flung her away from him like that?

There was no denying it. Brian Riegel complicated her life in a way no one else had ever been able to do. The thing that made it all the more confusing was that she seemed to want that complication.

You're not in love with him, she told herself firmly. *You're not!* There was no way she could be in love with a man she had barely carried on a conversation with. And it made no sense at all that what she felt might be the rebirth of the idealistic emotion of a teenager.

The ringing of the phone stopped her thoughts. Dawn fully expected to hear her mother when she picked up the receiver. Brian's deep voice caught her off guard. "What are you doing?" he asked.

"I'm digging my way out from under the mess, or at least I'm making an attempt at it. I swear I'm never going to get settled in," she said while trying to ignore the way her pulse had quickened at the sound of his voice.

"Do it later. I need you over at the field in ten minutes."

Dawn thought about the ragged cutoffs she'd

changed into after leaving her mother and cringed. "It's Sunday," she stalled. "I thought I was entitled to a day off."

"You get time off when I do. Ten minutes." He hung up without explaining further, leaving Dawn torn between wanting to call him back and inform him that she wasn't at his beck and call and knowing the day would have a hollow feel to it if she turned down a chance to be with him.

Five minutes later Dawn was getting into her car. She'd changed back into slacks and run a brush through her hair, which had decided to rebel against its present shampoo and become charged with electricity. As she backed out of the driveway she glanced in the rearview mirror and cringed. Her hair looked as if it should have weights tied to it to hold it under control, but if it bothered Brian, that was his problem. He surely couldn't expect her to run over to the field at a minute's notice, looking like she was ready for a night on the town. Not that he'd ever seen her really dressed up. That would truly be a shock—if he took note of her at all.

What hurt, despite her best efforts to hide the fact, was that since that one kiss Brian had acted as if Dawn was of no more consequence to her than the man who'd come to repaint the concession stand. Less. He had been full of talk about a river fishing trip, and Brian had listened attentively to his opinions about water temperatures and proper tackle.

Dawn didn't know what to expect when she pulled up just outside the main gate. Surely not the half dozen expensive cars, two of which sported out-of-state license plates.

Once she was inside, however, the pieces fell together. In addition to Brian, Verdue Field held Mathew Bishop, the vice-president of the franchise, who'd interviewed and then hired Dawn; a tall stocky man she vaguely recognized from televised baseball games; and several other distinguished gentlemen who looked oddly out of place in suits and ties on a baseball field. A strangely nervous Coach Weatherby hurried over to pull Dawn toward the group. "I wish I'd known they were all going to descend on us," he whispered to Dawn. "I sure as hell wasn't ready to have all the brass show up at one time."

"What are they doing here?" Dawn whispered back, but before the manager had a chance to reply, they were within earshot of the others. Dawn took little note of her presence as the only female in the group. Three days of working with the exuberant team of young ballplayers had quickly accustomed her to that. She smiled as Brian introduced her to the distinguished gentlemen and then the tall stocky man. That name rang a bell. He'd been managing professional baseball teams for years and was currently manager of the A's professional team. Dawn could barely hold her amusement in check. She couldn't count how many times she'd seen him on TV with a wad of tobacco pushing out his cheek. He looked definitely undressed without his trademark.

"I'm sorry to pull you out here on a Sunday," said the California-based manager she knew only as Mr. D. "But we're on a tight schedule. We found time to make a swing through the Rogue Valley between our other commitments. I'm afraid our farm teams sometimes feel we exist only as names on checks. The truth is, we're quite interested in how our potential future stars are doing."

"Will you be here long enough to watch their first game?" Dawn asked. The season was being launched in less than a week, and Dawn believed the ballplayers would be even more keyed up if they knew the men responsible for their employment were in the stands.

"I'm afraid not. You people"—he nodded at Brian— "are going to have to carry on without us. Not that that concerns us. Mr. Riegel here has taken care of everything."

If Brian felt any discomfort as a result of the compliment, he carried it off well. He simply made the comment that the local media, to say nothing of the county commissioners, had been quite accommodating. "I'll show you the features the newspaper has done on the Northwest League," he said. "I've received the most feedback from one the local paper did on Miss Morrell."

"Positive feedback, I assume," Mr. D. observed as the other men listened attentively.

"For the most part." Brian was staring at her, but Dawn couldn't read the message, if there was one, in his dark eyes. "There is some concern that a woman, a young woman yet, will be able to keep those young jocks in line."

Dawn's spine stiffened. Weren't they done with that issue yet? "I haven't been aware of any mass rebellion," she observed. "Granted, the idea of wind sprints hasn't met with total enthusiasm, but the players know the reason behind my orders. They've been doing this for years. But many had no idea why until I explained it to them."

"What about treatment facilities?" Mathew Bishop asked, and Dawn launched into an explanation of her efforts in that department. She explained that a treatment room was slowly taking form. It would include several complete weight lifting sets, in addition to the just-installed whirlpool bath—a vast improvement over what she'd begun with.

Dawn was pleased to see that a major thrust of the visit was a frank discussion of drug use by athletes and how this was viewed by the organization. Disclosure of drug use by Olympic potentials and professional athletes had made the franchise owners sensitive to any adverse publicity in that regard. They nodded approval when Dawn told them she'd made her position clear on that the first day. "In the long run it only hurts an athlete. I've passed out the results of studies showing that the use of amphetamines makes people think they're performing better than they actually are," she explained. "Uppers result in aggressive, hostile, and hyperactive behavior. When the drug wears off, depression sets in. It can become a vicious cycle."

"I'm impressed," Mr. D. observed. He turned toward the others. "I think we can be certain that Miss Morrell's thinking parallels our own. The last thing we need is some magazine or newspaper article pointing out one of our athletes as an addict."

Brian had stood silent while this was going on, but now he spoke. "Miss Morrell seems to feel it's necessary to make herself an example for the others to follow. She's been out there every morning, jogging around the field with the players. For all I know she lifts weights too."

Was that meant as a criticism? If Brian was trying to put her down because she'd shown up wearing running shoes in contrast to the men's ties, she was sorry, but ten minutes wasn't much advance notice.

"As a matter of fact, I do lift weights," she said. "Contrary to lingering myths, women don't become muscle bound when they get involved in weight training. They just increase their strength. I don't see anything wrong in a woman being able to hold her own. Besides, there are obvious health advantages."

Before she could stop him, Brian grabbed her arm. His fingers wrapped easily around it. "You're right. You aren't muscle bound. You look like you'd blow away in a stiff wind. Besides, I don't think anyone is really interested in whether you pump iron or not."

"You're the one who brought it up," she shot back. She thought about pulling away, but Brian might think his touch had unsettled her. She clamped her lips together, eyes flashing. She was determined to remain passively in his grip until he tired of his game. The conversation had turned to an as yet unsettled agreement with the vendor who would be running the concession stand. Brian was concentrating on answering the owners' questions, but his hand remained possessively on Dawn's arm as if daring her to dismiss its presence.

It wasn't until Brian invited the men into his office that she was free. Dawn clenched her fist, ridding her flesh of the impression his fingers had made. His crack about her physical fitness program was uncalled for, but as she trailed after the men there was no denying that she was impressed by Brian's manner. He walked with casual assurance in the midst of the rich and powerful men who were capable of molding baseball franchises. He'd come a long way from the jock who, as far as she knew or cared in those days, lived from one game to another.

"What about meeting with the press?" Mathew Bishop was asking. "Do you want to fill us in on that, Brian?"

"The groundwork has been laid," Brian replied. "I decided we needed more than a press conference. After all, what we do this spring is going to provide a lot of copy for the media. Several members of the press indicated they wanted to do more than just shake your hands. The Red Lion Inn cocktail room has been reserved for tomorrow night. Invitations went out to members of the press from the newspaper and TV stations. Since the games will be carried over one of our local radio stations, I took the liberty of extending an invitation to their staff also."

Mathew Bishop shrugged his shoulders, nodding vigorously at the same time. "Then it's all set. I should have known you'd have things in hand, Brian." He turned toward Dawn. "It wouldn't be complete without the one female member of the organization. You are coming, aren't you, Miss Morrell?"

It was all Dawn could do to keep her mouth from dropping open. Brian had been planning a cocktail party with the top brass for some time now. And yet he hadn't told her. She knew enough of the man to realize it wasn't a simple oversight on his part.

Didn't he want her there? Dawn's head came up in rebellion. Maybe Brian didn't want her around, but she was part of the organization. She had as much right to attend this gathering as anyone else, she knew. "I wouldn't miss it," she acknowledged. "Should I wear my best tux, or something more ordinary?"

"It's going to be fairly informal," Brian supplied. "You can wear anything you want, as long as you change out of running shoes. A baseball jersey would be more casual than we had in mind. I'm hoping you can dress yourself without my help."

"I'll try to remember that," she said spiritedly, even though her heart was in her mouth. What had she done wrong?

A few minutes later she thought she had an answer, at least one that felt better than the possibility that Brian didn't want to be around her. The men had filed out with Coach Weatherby, who'd promised to take them on a tour that included the older downtown hotel where the ballplayers who hadn't yet found other accommodations were staying.

Brian was on the phone the moment the door closed behind the men. Dawn stood, uncomfortable, wondering whether she should take this as a sign of her dismissal and yet reluctant to leave.

"I'm planning on picking him up in the afternoon," Brian was saying. "The boy needs new shoes. I know what I want him to wear. After all, I'm paying for them."

Dawn backed away from the taut look on Brian's face and reached for the doorknob. This conversation was private. She had no intention of eavesdropping on something that had to be settled between Brian and his ex-wife. She headed outside and toward her car, shaken because she hadn't been prepared for the heavy anger smoldering in Brian's eyes.

She settled into her car and rested her head on the steering wheel. Why did life have to be so complicated? If only she didn't have this urge to place her arms around Brian's shoulders and show him that she understood how he must feel about having to fight for any involvement in his son's life. But Brian was accustomed to handling this alone. He didn't want a gesture from her, and if she gave it, it would only bring her more pain. Better to forget it, leave Brian to live his own life. Besides, it was time for her to branch out in the community and develop a network of friends she could depend on. Maybe she'd even go somewhere where she might meet a man.

"I thought you'd left. Don't you want to hurry home and start getting ready for tomorrow?"

Dawn jumped at the unexpected words. She looked out through the open car window. Brian's face was a shadowy image because of the sun. "The party isn't until tomorrow," she observed. "I don't think it'll take that long to get presentable." She took a deep breath, relieved that she had to squint to see him at all. It made it possible to forget how appealing she found Brian's face. "You didn't want me there, did you?"

"What makes you say that?"

"I'm not ignorant, Brian. Why didn't you let me know earlier? The press got their invitations. I'm sure Coach Weatherby knew all about it. I'm the only one who didn't know our bosses were going to be in the valley. Did you think I was going to embarrass you in some way?"

"Ralph is going to be there."

"What does he have to do with this?" she demanded. "My God, you don't think I'm afraid of facing him, do you? He's going to behave himself with all those people there."

"What you and Ralph do is none of my concern."

Why did he have to sound so cold? It made carrying on a rational conversation nearly impossible. "What is that supposed to mean?"

"Can't you figure it out? Ralph can be a very persuasive man. It isn't impossible that you've become aware of his charms."

Despite herself Dawn laughed. "Ralph is an animal." Did Brian really believe she saw anything attractive in the overbearing man? "I hoped you had a higher opinion of me," she said softly. "At one time I had very good taste in men."

"That was a long time ago." Brian started to back up and then stopped. "I won't be seeing my son this week."

"I'm sorry." Suddenly Dawn forgot her conflicting feelings. Instinctively she placed her hand over Brian's. "Is there anything I can do?"

"I doubt it. That's what I have a lawyer for." Brian pulled his hand away. "I don't need your input, thank you. I have all the advice I can use."

Dawn shrank away. The bitterness in his voice had effectively sealed the words in her throat. Blindly she reached for her keys, wanting nothing more than to get away from this man.

She didn't get that far. Brian reached in through the window and took her chin in his hands. She had no choice but to turn toward him. As she lifted her head he dipped his body and gently brushed his lips against her own exposed ones.

She stopped breathing, stopped thinking. Maybe her heart itself stopped beating. Dawn didn't know. The only thing she could possibly be aware of was the whispering sensuous feeling of his warm lips against hers. They were neither demanding nor promising. If any statement was made it was simply that this moment existed.

"Go home." He pulled away, robbing her. "Be glad you never married."

Dawn drove home in a daze. There was simply no understanding Brian Riegel. If the man was trying to throw her off-balance, he certainly was doing a credible job of it. Or at least he'd succeed if she didn't get control of herself.

Insanity lay in allowing herself to be vulnerable. A kiss was just that, a kiss. Someday, maybe, she'd try to sort out the reason for it. But not now. She had a party to think about, an impression to make with the men who'd hired her. And an impression to make with Brian.

Dawn knew what she was doing when she took the dress off its hanger the next afternoon. The winter-white knit clung softly over her flat stomach and slim hips to reveal long slender legs. The elbow-length sleeves were slit at the top so that the fabric draped and let her upper arms show. It wasn't belted but rather slid down her body in an unbroken line. The dress was perfect for late afternoon cocktails when a feminine statement was needed, but that wasn't why Dawn wore it.

One night ten years ago Dawn had worn white. She was doing it again. Her hair, lightly blow-dried and allowed to feather against her neck and shoulders, was almost one in color with the dress. If she hadn't been so deeply tanned, the effect would have been too stark, but as Dawn applied lipstick and a touch of mascara she admitted that her flesh had just enough color to carry off the understated dress and hair.

An angel, Brian had called her. Would he remember? she wondered.

The intimate cocktail room of the Red Lion Inn was already filled when Dawn entered. She'd been aware of the appreciative glance from the inn employee who'd directed her to the room, but she had no recollection of what he looked like. What would he think if he knew that for months she'd carried a metal screw firmly attached to her fibula? It wasn't a pretty thought, but without the support the screw had provided during a critical period in her recovery, she probably wouldn't now be able to push open the solid door and glide through.

Dawn stood motionless, waiting for her eyes to accustom themselves to the dim light cast by muted overhead fixtures and several candles stationed throughout a room dominated by a circular gas fireplace. Because the late afternoon was warm, the gas logs hadn't been lit, but people still tended to gravitate around the structure. Before Dawn could decide on a course of action she felt her elbow being taken and turned to take in the wiry, if short, phsyique of Coach Weatherby.

"Quite a bash, don't you think?" he said under cover of the sound of a dozen conversations. "Frankly, I'm more at home with beer and pizza, but if they're willing to pay for it, who am I to complain? I'll get you a drink." He stopped talking and gave her a long look. "Don't ever let the kids see you in that dress. They'll never think of baseball again."

"Coach, you're impossible." Dawn laughed. She'd liked the manager's down-to-earth attitude from the day she met him. The fact that he was old enough to be her father added to the positive feelings she had for him. "Is there any wine? I'm not much of a drinker."

"You bet. I don't mind women drinking, but there's nothing wrong with a little restraint." He patted his stomach. "Stay away from beer if you don't want to wind up with a belly to fight."

Dawn followed after the manager as he made his way to the corner bar and said something to the bartender that Dawn didn't catch. A moment later he handed her a half-filled long-stemmed glass. "Is white wine all right? I wouldn't like to see Burgundy spilled on that dress. That's a real knockout. Who are you trying to impress?"

"Does it look like that?" Dawn asked, concerned. "I don't have many dressy outfits. I didn't have much to choose from."

"Don't let me rattle you," the manager reassured her. "You look great. In fact, if Mr. Riegel doesn't notice, he's not the man I thought he was."

"I don't think Mr. Riegel cares what I wear," Dawn said as calmly as she could.

"That, my dear, may be something we'll never know. It hasn't been an easy year for Brian. His wife quite frankly kicked him in the teeth, especially where the boy is concerned. I don't think he's recovered yet."

Dawn wasn't sure whether she wanted Coach

Weatherby to continue the conversation or not, but obviously he didn't feel he was telling any tales out of school. "I knew Brian casually before he and his wife separated. That was after they moved back here," he explained. "When you're involved in sports in this part of the state, your paths are bound to cross. Anyway, I thought it strange that he never mentioned her. He'd bring his son up every time he had a chance. I remember seeing him at a football game with the little guy wrapped up in one of those sleeper things with the zipper when he was just learning to talk. That was one guy who didn't run the other way when it was baby-sitting time. He'd show up at the darnedest places with the little fellow hanging on to his thumb, and he'd run to him every time he fell down and skinned his knees. Like I said, his wife didn't seem to be much in his life. She was getting started in business or something, so I figured she was on a trip. You know how it is when you're getting your foot back in the door after being out of state a few years. You take work a lot more seriously than when you're settled in comfortably."

Dawn nodded.

"Anyway, it didn't surprise me much when it came out that Brian and his wife weren't living together anymore. I understand he isn't happy with the custody agreement. It wouldn't surprise me if he gets custody of Tad one of these days. Still, I don't think that is an easy decision for Brian. I mean, even with all this equality for the sexes these days, I think most men still believe young kids belong with their mothers. But that boy is his life."

Almost as if the words were a trigger, Dawn located

Brian. He was in a far corner of the room, surrounded by three of the gentlemen Dawn had met yesterday. As Coach Weatherby switched gears and launched into a monologue of his opinion of Ralph and his sometimes slapdash reporting, Dawn watched Brian from under hooded eyes. He was concentrating on what was being said to him and yet seemed to be holding himself apart at the same time. It didn't take Dawn long to realize why. Brian was looking around the room for something—or someone.

She hadn't had time to drop her eyes when his met hers across the man-made shadows. Their eyes locked, cementing a nameless bond despite the distance between them. Dawn lost all sense of the others in the room. Coach Weatherby was still talking, but it could have been in a foreign tongue for all the sense it made.

Brian was looking at her, and that's all her heart had room for. His expression gave no indication of his feelings, but the shock of being locked visually with Brian made it impossible for her to question the significance of his carefully neutral expression. How long they remained with their eyes riveted together Dawn couldn't guess. She didn't care. The moment could go on forever.

But then his eyes released her and she stood, swaying, as his eyes made their way down her body. He'd seen the white dress, the white backdrop of her hair. Did it stir him, take him back those ten years?

When again he met her gaze, his own gave away no secrets. His eyes were carefully guarded. Once again, for a timeless stretch, she was a prisoner in his grip. When at last he broke it off, she felt as if she'd been stripped of all strength.

"I think maybe that's too much wine," Coach Weatherby was saying. "The blood's gone to your cheeks."

"Has it?" Dawn touched her cheeks and found them flushing. "I—I'm sorry."

"For what? For enjoying yourself? Come on, girl. You know any small talk? I think we're supposed to mingle. Make ourselves accessible, so to speak."

Only the manager's callused hand against the small of her back gave Dawn the necessary push to command her feet to move. She made her way back to the bar, where a couple of TV newsmen were talking. She allowed Coach Weatherby to take the lead in the conversation, commenting only minimally. It didn't surprise her to find that the topic was baseball. She forced herself to concentrate and soon found herself poking fun at her childhood attempts to compete with the boys. She admitted to a lack of strength necessary to hit the ball far enough to get it out of the infield. "I was always so grateful when I was walked," she admitted. "Otherwise I'd never get to first."

"You don't need to compete with the boys on the diamond these days," Ralph said as he came up behind her. He put a possessive hand on her shoulder and drew her firmly against him. "You dress like that, and they'll let you get away with anything. There's a lot more woman under those jerseys you're always wearing than you let on."

Dawn pulled away. She gave Ralph a look designed to be both a warning and suggestive of a peace agreement. "Have you seen my cleats? These shoes are killing me. I'd like to slip into something more comfortable."

"Don't change a thing. We jaded old businessmen need to look at something feminine once in a while," Dawn heard someone say, and turned to face one of the men Brian had been talking to a minute ago. A silent Brian was in tow. "Not enough women wear dresses these days. It's like a breath of spring, don't you think, Brian?" the man asked.

Brian worked his jaw before speaking. "You wear white a lot."

"I'm sorry to hear you object to that. I happen to like it." Dawn was surprised to find her voice had its usual strength.

Brian didn't answer. Instead, he turned toward the bartender and asked for a refill on his drink. As the conversation once again picked up Dawn noticed that Brian barely touched the drink in his broad hand and wondered why he'd ordered another. Her own glass of wine was becoming warm, but since she had little interest in it, she continued to twirl it slowly in her fingers. The conversation was again back to business, specifically the launching of the season. Brian introduced the A's owners to the man who was going to do the radio broadcasting and brought them up to date on the background information the man had on each ballplayer. "Chuck has been broadcasting local high school and college sports for years. He doesn't need me trying to tell him what to do."

Dawn tried to shake the cobwebs out of her head without it appearing obvious. Why was it that Brian's voice was the only one that was coming in clearly? She was acutely aware of his every gesture, of the careful way he shifted weight as if favoring one knee. She didn't think anyone else was aware of that, but because she was closely attuned to him, nothing he did or said escaped her.

An hour later no one seemed disposed to break up the gathering. Through general agreement the group moved into the dining room and claimed two large round tables. Dawn found herself situated between Coach Weatherby and Brian, with Ralph directly across from her. Although it was made clear that the tab would be picked up by the organization, Dawn settled for a light soufflé. She knew she wouldn't have much of an appetite, not with Brian so near.

But he was ignoring her, his conversation directed toward Mathew Bishop. Dawn would have given anything to be possessed of the same self-control, but it was impossible. Because of the cramped quarters, her bare forearm kept brushing against the sleeve of Brian's shirt. The white collar of his shirt stood out in contrast to his dark hair and gave even more depth to his eyes. He'd left the top buttons open for comfort, but what it showed of his strong chest was undeniably distracting. The sight of Brian formally attired reawakened memories of Dawn's wool-smelling father as he took his leave of his family in the morning. Brian's clothes were less traditional, but they bespoke comfortable self-assurance, a professional man at home in the company of his peers.

And yet this was the same man who could hoist a child onto his hip and absorb an ice-cream stained face in a kiss. Dawn shuddered, helpless to fight the impact this knowledge made with her senses. Brian was more, much more than these men could fathom. He was both competent and compassionate—at least compassionate with his son. She didn't know what the truth was where she was concerned. Or maybe she did and was unable to face that fact.

As the others kept the conversation going Dawn concentrated on her meal and the warmth radiating from the man to her left. His arm brushed hers gently, stirring the finely spun hairs on her shoulders and sending an electric current coursing through her. She no longer fought to keep abreast of the topic but allowed her mind to focus on what was happening to her senses. As once again his sleeve came in contact with her, she admitted what couldn't be denied. If it hadn't been for this public place, for her fragile grasp on civilization, Dawn Morrell would have revealed her deepest secret to Brian Riegel. She was a woman. He was a man. That was all there was.

Dawn wouldn't have been able to make any comment about her dinner. It was tasteless, and eating only an automatic gesture. She was transported into a world of sensual experiences, willing, eager even to taste the full benefit of what his touch was doing to her. And yet by all outward appearances Dawn was a woman whose attention had been perhaps slightly dulled by wine but was certainly nothing more than a quiet member of the group.

She even entered into the discussion of how to best work off the effects of a full meal. Coach Weatherby mentioned that the inn had a live band this week and that dancing was encouraged. "If Dawn doesn't mind a variety of partners, I think we'd all rather do that than go jogging dressed like we are," the manager observed, and pulled Dawn to her feet before she could object.

The inn's Blue Room was smaller than the dining

area but well arranged for dancing. The band was a trio made up of piano, guitar, and violin, performing on a raised stage. Small intimate tables were lined up around the edges with a well-polished wooden floor for dancing in the center. Recessed ceiling lights cast a bluish glow over the room. Although Dawn had never been here before, she'd seen the room advertised in the paper's entertainment section. She hadn't done much dancing since Jim's accident, and her body ached with the need to give physical expression to the spell the music was driving through her.

At first she danced with the manager and Mathew Bishop, laughing at their comic approach to gallant manners. She even managed to bite back an exclamation as Coach Weatherby accidently crushed her toes under his. As her partners changed to other members of the organization's hierarchy, she realized that they were merging in her mind until she wasn't sure how many of them she'd danced with. She attempted to locate Brian in the dim room, but when she did his back was to her and he was deep in conversation with Ralph. That disturbed her, although she was hard pressed to know why.

More than once she was asked whether she was tiring, but Dawn was operating on pure adrenaline. The guitar had the power to charge her body with a seemingly endless source of energy. Now that Brian's distracting presence had been removed, she found that her body had become a sponge, soaking up both rhythm and sound. She could literally dance the night away, and like an addict high on drugs, she saw her changing partners only as a socially accepted outlet for the restlessness coursing through her.

She closed her eyes because she didn't want the distraction of everyday things and let the music take her to that floating place where the years no longer had any weight. Dawn was a girl again, a questing teenager with love blooming for the first time. She could look at a boy and see a dream future instead of reality. Brian Riegel was the embodiment of everything a girl reaching for womanhood dreams of. He was Prince Charming waiting to whisk her off to his castle for a future of nothing more substantial than rose blossoms and cloudless mornings. How innocent that time had been, how full of promise! There'd been no reason to dwell on the mundane details that absorb all adults. She could give in to her dreams, to the man capable of giving those dreams shape.

Her arms emptied and filled again as yet another man took her in his arms. She barely glanced at him, so deep was she in the past. But slowly her arms told her the story. She was no longer in the grip of a middle-aged man who handled her as if she were a child entrusted to his care. The man holding her was a male of today, the embodiment of masculinity—of sensuality even.

Dawn opened her eyes. She didn't start when she recognized Brian. With the deep blue shadows to protect her, she found the courage to meet his gaze, to keep her eyes locked on his. Her body molded perfectly against his, the smaller feminine form tight in the grip of masculinity. His muscles were hard but not overpoweringly demanding. Rather they possessed her naturally as if these two separate humans had been made to fit together.

Slowly, peacefully, Dawn let her chin drop and

broke the eye contact. She brought her head forward until it was resting in the nest of his shoulder. Once again she blocked out the world. It was as if she knew that this moment was precious beyond price. If it never happened again, she would need its memory to sustain her for all the years to come. *Brian,* her heart whispered. *Brian. Is there, could there ever be anyone else?*

She felt his lips softly caressing the spun whiteness of her fine hair and cried silently with the joy it gave her.

"Remember the guitar?" she whispered. She was unaware that she'd spoken aloud until she heard the words. "There was one that night."

"I remember."

Again she fell silent. If she could have willed this moment to last forever, she knew she would never again ask for anything. Brian was holding her in his arms. There were no defenses between them, no barriers. That might come again in the morning, but this was tonight.

"Do you remember what you called me?" she ventured.

"An angel. A white angel."

Dawn had almost again surrendered to the spell when Brian pushed her gently away from him. She was held fast in fingers that barely marred the surface of her exposed forearms. "Why did you have to wear white tonight?"

Chapter Seven

Dawn looked up into Brian's blazing eyes and acknowledged a shudder tracing itself down the length of her body. "I—what do you mean? What's wrong?"

"You know damn well what's wrong! You wore white when you came to that party." He held her rigid and yet in such a way that Dawn was sure none of the others was aware of the tension that existed between them. "Why the hell did you have to pull a stunt like that?"

"I'm not trying to pull any stunt!" She jerked back against his punishing fingers but couldn't break free. "What do you care what I wear? Our bosses seem to like it," she pointed out. "I'd think you'd approve."

"Angel?" He laughed bitterly. "Devil is more like it. You know what you're doing all right. But it isn't going to work. I'm not going to fall for any innocent act." For a moment taut silence hung between them as Dawn was subjected to the full force of Brian's anger. She wondered if she might faint when, instead of shaking her or flinging her from him, he captured her lips with his own demanding ones. The force of his mouth bearing down on her was like a physical blow. But this blow reached more than her mouth. Its impact touched her heart.

His kiss, punishing as it was, filled a need Dawn had already been aware of no matter how much she fought to deny its existence. In her present state she would have welcomed any contact with Brian, even this cruel one. She needed him. There was no denying that. Dawn's entire body responded, surging to life. Despite every shred of sanity left in her, she found herself responding to him. She found her way into the circle of his arms, her breasts crushed against the buttons of his shirt. She felt the firmness of his thighs against hers, their warmth coursing a path through both heather-tone trousers and white knit.

She closed her eyes against what she might see on his face and took what pleasure she could from his sudden kiss. She knew all too well that he might never touch her again.

Then just as suddenly as he'd accepted the physical contact, he forced her from him. "Devil!" he hissed under cover of the music. "Devil in an angel's dress!"

He was gone, a blurred figure making its way to the exit and in that move stripping the room of life. Dawn swayed, barely able to stand, alone in the middle of the dance floor. She pressed her lids tight against her eyes in an effort to shake off the light-headedness that threatened to envelop her. As if aware of her state, Coach Weatherby grabbed her around the waist and gave her his shoulder for support. "Problems?" he asked.

Dawn started to shake her head, then realized she was incapable of fabricating a story for the condition her emotions were in. "I—I don't know what I did wrong," she moaned. "I have no idea where I stand with Brian."

The manager only grinned. "I think that's a pretty accurate assessment of his state of mind these days. Come on, kid. I'm buying you a real drink this time. You need it."

Dawn didn't argue. She let him lead her to an empty table and then silently accepted the mixed drink he placed in her trembling hands. Her eyes kept straying to the door, but whether in anticipation or fear she didn't know. She felt dimly the need to break the silence, but speech took more self-control than she had.

Fortunately Coach Weatherby didn't seem to be disturbed by her tongue-tied state. He leaned toward her so his voice would carry and began. "Forgive an old man butting in, but you look like you need to let down your hair around someone. Brian told me you two knew each other a long time ago. Tonight wouldn't have anything to do with that, would it?"

"I honestly don't know," she admitted. "He brought it up. Did he ever! I think that what I'm wearing, the music, reminded him of that." She couldn't tell the manager that her outfit wasn't all innocence. Some things she had a need to keep to herself. "But why did he treat me that way?" Her voice broke and she had to bite her lip to keep from crying.

"Because that man has his head on backward these days when it comes to women," Coach Weatherby observed. "I think it's safe to say that the woman he was married to put him through a lot. I don't know for sure, but I've heard it said she has a lapful of emotional hang-ups. If that's the case, she's done a creditable job of trying to push them off onto Brian.''

"But he's divorced," Dawn managed.

"Yes, he is. But there's still his son. He doesn't have the boy free from that craziness yet."

"Yet?"

"Didn't Brian tell you? He's fighting for custody of Tad. The boy's mother's family has money, and she's fighting with a high-priced lawyer. I think Brian will win in the end, but it's a pretty dirty battle these days. I know Brian's determined to keep his nose clean."

"What do you mean?" Dawn didn't think she'd be able to think of anything save her shattered nerves, but there was an intense look on the manager's face, plus the drink was warming her back to life. Maybe Brian was entitled to a certain privacy, but like it or not she was involved. She had to know where Brian's life was heading.

"I mean her lawyer is fighting dirty. If Brian so much as looks at another woman, he's afraid that'll be the end of his chance of getting his son. Also, well, I think what went on when he was married made him pretty cynical when it comes to women."

He doesn't want anything to do with women, Dawn thought, the realization hitting her between the eyes. She'd suspected it before but cast off the thought because it was too painful to admit. "He said his son was the most important thing in his life. Tad is the only person he loves."

"Don't be so sure, kid." Coach Weatherby patted her hand. "Given the right woman, any man can change his mind about being a recluse. You're kind of rangy, like a colt. But there's nothing wrong with that."

Dawn only shook her head. "If Brian cared anything for me, he wouldn't have done what he did tonight. I can't talk to him. I don't know why I should even try."

Dawn's conviction took her through the night and into the next morning. She slept only in fits and starts and woke early with a headache she knew couldn't have come from what little she'd had to drink. Although she went jogging as soon as she'd put on some clothes, the hour spent running through the quiet streets did little to revive her spirit. She'd taken a shower and was putting away the fated white dress when she made her decision. Brian didn't want anything to do with her. How much clearer did he have to make it than what he'd done last night? she asked herself. She wasn't going to continue to play the fool. Back her heart would go into that protective sheeting that had sustained it over the years.

What caused the problem was that she was clinging to the past, not letting go of youthful fantasies. That's what had brought on her present heartache. But it couldn't continue this way. Dawn was determined to draw a curtain over the boy and girl who'd shared one magic night and live with the reality of today. From now on she was determined to see Brian for what he was—the general manager of the farm team playing in the Northwest League, and a man embroiled in a custody battle that had soured him on romance.

And if her heart still didn't understand?

That was something Dawn was going to have to deal with in private. What her heart felt would have to remain her secret until she'd gained better control over it. Love? It was only a word. A word that could be erased from the heart just as it could be erased from a page. Brian made it as plain as possible. He didn't want her playing in his ball park.

Dawn had her emotions firmly in check by the time the Northwest League formally opened its season. Although it hadn't been in her job description, Dawn had pitched in wherever needed, running down the manager of the athletic supply store and impressing him with the need to have lettering on the uniforms printed and ready for opening day ceremonies. She even accompanied Brian to two tentative advertisers and contributed to Brian's sales pitch to the point where both businessmen were now committed to promoting baseball as part of their radio advertising program. The venture had cost Dawn dearly in emotional control, but because Brian was distant and impersonal, she'd somehow managed to submerge her feelings and concentrate on their objective.

The weeks, months really, of planning were over. For the most part Dawn was satisfied with the team's commitment to her training program and felt able to maintain their physical condition throughout the season. She chafed somewhat because Big Bob continued to make light of her suggestion that he should cut down on his use of salt. The bullish man obviously believed he was the final authority on everything and either turned a deaf ear or made sarcastic remarks when Dawn was talking to the players about essential nutrients.

But Big Bob was the exception. To her relief she found she hadn't had to work that hard at proving herself an authority in the field of sports medicine. She rather suspected it was a combination of being able to back up her statements with facts and the players' desire to do everything possible to increase their chance of making it into the pro ranks.

Now it was Tuesday, opening day. The day took on particular significance as soon as she glanced at the calendar. She would be traveling with the team when they went on the road to play, but today was for Verdue Field. The structure that had become a symbol of sports activity in this part of the state was cleaned and groomed, ready for its entry into the world of professional baseball—even if at a farm team level.

Dawn arrived at Verdue Field early, not because she had that much to do before the game, but because she was too nervous to continue to pace in her suddenly too-small house. Her mother had called earlier to confirm that she and Peter would be on hand to lend moral support. "I really don't have much idea what you're doing," Crystal admitted. "You have to point out everyone you've been talking about. Especially Brian Riegel."

Dawn's reserve to spend opening day attending to business wavered at that, but as she entered Verdue Field she knew she'd be able to hold in check any distracting thoughts of the general manager. Vendors were setting up in the concession stands. The college students hired to maintain the field were busy watering down the base paths and infield prior to chalking the lines, but fans hadn't yet started to arrive.

Dawn loved Verdue Field during this period of anticipation. It was almost as if the complex were capable of breathing its own breath, of becoming more than grass and stands and wire fencing. Like a circus spreading its big tent for the night's performance, the field stood ready, pulsing with anticipation. As Dawn stood looking down on the diamond itself she remembered the day when she ran the bases. Today the impulse was back again.

She turned at the sound of metal cleats on cement and found herself face to face with Big Bob. "Are you ready for this?" he asked. "It isn't the Oakland Coliseum, but it'll have to do for this year. Then it's on up the ladder for me."

"You sound pretty confident," Dawn observed. Was that a hint of liquor she smelled on his breath?

"You better believe it, lady." Big Bob grinned. "This is one man who knows where he's heading. I'm not about to spend any more time in the bush leagues than absolutely necessary. I've already got myself an agent. He's going to make damn sure the top brass knows I'm here—and ready to move up."

"That's pretty rarefied air you're talking about," Dawn tried to point out. She had her doubts that Bob would listen to her, but in the few weeks she'd been working for the organization she'd become aware of how few promising young men ever made it into the pro ranks. Athletic ability wasn't always enough. There had to be that extra something—a spark or drive that set one man apart from the others. Bob had confidence, but Dawn wasn't sure he was capable of making the immediate sacrifices necessary for the longtime goal. His love of nightlife and lackluster attitude toward training and conditioning were only symptoms of his underlying attitude.

"And I'm going to breathe that air. Don't you ever

doubt that, lady," Bob went on. "Today's just the start." At the sound of others coming out of the dressing room Bob shrugged and turned toward them. "Time to join the kids. The trouble with most of them is they're still wet behind the ears."

Dawn stared after Bob, biting her lower lip as she studied his swaggering walk. Just because she didn't like Bob's attitude was insufficient proof on which to hang her gut feeling that the arrogant young man was heading for trouble. What was it, then?

She had little time to spend thinking about Big Bob. When she saw Coach Weatherby coming out of the locker room, she joined the team and led them through their loosening-up exercises. As she moved among the players, making suggestions and asking about a tight muscle here or a weak ankle there, she was aware of the growing volume of sound as the stands filled up. Like an orchestra tuning up, the sound took on added dimension. Verdue Field was launching its season. These people had come for the performance.

And she was part of the show.

"This is really the place to be," she told a strangely untalkative manager as the teams were getting ready to go onto the field for the national anthem. "No one can see us down here in the dugouts."

"You hiding from something?" Coach Weatherby asked.

She shook her head, although aware that Brian was somewhere in the press booth. "I just don't like having a lot of people looking at me." She pasted a teasing smile on her face. "Basically, I'm a shy child."

Dawn wasn't given long to hide. Through an uneventful first inning she sat on a far corner of the bench and watched the action. Unless someone was injured, she had no real task during the actual games and could simply enjoy her front row seat. As a life-long baseball fan, she was looking forward to nothing more than a spring evening game under the lights when she heard her name being called from the top of the steps leading into the dugout.

"Are you planning on hibernating in there? There are other ways you can make yourself useful."

Dawn started at Brian's critical tones but quickly gained hold of her emotions. She refused to let her eyes linger on his trim terry pullover shirt and corduroy jeans. "I'm sorry if I've done something to offend you, Mr. Riegel. But I'm not aware of any tasks I've left undone."

"You've rolled all your bandages, have you? Come here, then. I have need of you." He jerked his head to indicate the press box.

Dawn started to protest, but it was clear that Brian wasn't in any mood for argument. As she joined him, she became aware of the subtle change in his usually relaxed manner. It wasn't that he was nervous. Dawn couldn't say that of him. Rather he was alert, on call, tuned to any unanticipated need that might come up.

As he took her elbow and steered her past the rows of seats and up the stairs leading to the press box, she could feel the barely controlled electrical charge within him. He seemed to be stepping slower than customary up the stairs, but it might have been because he was carefully scanning the seats. "The county commissioners are here," he whispered to her. "They received minority, but well-organized opposition to our selling beer, but in the end they voted with the field. I want them to know we appreciate their stand. Beer is traditional with ball parks, to say nothing of it being financially profitable.''

Dawn didn't know whether he expected a response, but just as she was turning toward him, he dropped her elbow to shake hands with a gentleman sitting in an aisle seat. Dawn was introduced to the mayor and his wife and even managed not to flush when the mayor's wife carried on about how it was time women were being recognized as capable of performing in any capacity.

If Dawn had any hope that the matter of her sex in an untraditional role no longer attracted attention, she learned differently when she was informed of her reason for being in the press box. The announcer doing the play by play for the radio station had requested a short interview with Dawn to be carried out between innings. Dawn shot a trapped and angry look at Brian, but he only smiled before turning her over to the announcer.

The interview went about as well as could be expected, although Dawn cringed as repeated and unnecessary, she felt, reference was made to her pale hair and surfer tan. The man also asked her age and then asked his unseen audience if they could believe that such a young woman had commanded the respect of an entire ball team. "I have it from good authority that she's doing a creditable job," he continued. "The general manager, Brian Riegel, admits that he had his reservations, but so far he hasn't seen any sign of insecurity on Miss Morrell's part." For her own part Dawn did her best to come across as someone who knew her job. Not only did she answer the questions in detail, but she added comments about a squeeze play and the infield fly rule. When the announcer responded, there was respect in his voice.

Finally, Dawn was released. She hurried from the section reserved for the electronic equipment needed by members of the press and pushed her way out the door. She glanced around, looking for Brian, but he had disappeared. *That's right,* she thought. *Turn me over to the lions and then leave.*

She was barely aware of the angry slapping sound her shoes made on the cement steps until she'd reached the ground level. Then she heard her name being called and turned to see her mother and Peter sitting just behind home plate in the seats she'd reserved for them. Dawn squeezed in next to her mother. "What do you think? Is Verdue Field going to be a success?" she asked.

"Do you even have to ask? My dear, I don't know when I've had so much fun." Her mother grinned. "It feels like the circus has come to town. Everyone is having a wonderful time. I can't get over it. My little girl is part of all this."

"Your little girl is pushing thirty," Dawn pointed out.

"Don't remind me." Crystal wrinkled up her nose. "You know how old that makes me, don't you? Never mind. By the way, I met your general manager. He came over and said he knew I was your mother. Asked if we liked our seats and could he do anything for us. Honey, he's just right for the job. He's self-confident and friendly at the same time. He takes time to talk to everyone, to make sure they feel right at home."

Was she really talking about the silent stranger

who'd hauled her out of the dugout a few minutes ago? "I'm glad you're impressed," Dawn observed. "That's his public face. I happen to know there's another side to him."

"Oh?" Crystal looked puzzled. "You're going to have to tell me about that when you have more time. All I can say is that I took an instant liking to him. He seems impressed with what you're doing too."

"Too bad he can't bring himself to tell me that," Dawn snapped as she got up. She left without seeing the puzzled look on her mother's face.

Thanks to a fast-moving game that resulted in a 7–6 win for the home team, Dawn had little time to ponder her mother's reaction to Brian. Of course, Crystal was unaware that Dawn had been shoved into an interview without her consent, but just the same, Dawn would have felt better if she'd known her mother was on her side. Other than putting an ice pack on a knee jammed during a slide into third, Dawn's only concern was one she shared with the manager in regard to Big Bob. "He's awfully keyed up and excitable. And he isn't concentrating the way he should," Coach Weatherby said about the team's second baseman. "Damn fool. I don't like sounding suspicious, but I'm willing to bet that if we ran a blood test, we'd find uppers in his system."

Dawn nodded. "His timing is off. I'm sure he isn't aware of that. He probably thinks he's doing a superior job."

"The only thing he's going to do is screw up his chances of a future in baseball if he doesn't wise up," was the final comment the manager made.

As soon as possible after the game Dawn sought

out her mother. She found Crystal and Peter waiting not far outside the team's locker room. "Do you go in there with them?" Crystal asked.

"Not so far." Dawn laughed. "If the time comes when someone's bleeding to death, I guess I'll have to plunge in. But I'm going to respect their privacy. I think it pays off in them respecting me. What do you think of what we're doing here? Do you think people are going to continue to come to the games?"

Peter placed an arm around Dawn's shoulders. "You have a winner here, young lady. People want to be out of doors this time of year. What better way to spend a warm evening than going to a ball game? I don't think anything is ever going to take over baseball as the all-American sport."

Dawn had wondered what her reaction would be when and if Peter Tinseth started acting as if he were a member of the family. She was pleased to realize that his arm around her had a natural feel. "Thank you. I hope enough people share your views," she said. When she first accepted the job offer, she hadn't thought she'd be concerned with the financial success of the operation as long as the organization paid her salary, but she now realized she'd become involved in much more than just the physical health of the men entrusted to her. How much Brian had to do with that attitude she wasn't going to think about.

Peter and Crystal tried to talk Dawn into having a late dinner with them, but because there was a morning practice scheduled, she begged off. By the time they left, Verdue Field was nearly deserted.

Dawn stood gazing out at the expensive field lights that bathed the diamond in light long after the sun had gone down. Moths and an occasional bat or owl flew erratically near the lights, bringing a flickering quality to the night. Although it was almost uncomfortably cool by now, Dawn was reluctant to leave. By day Verdue Field had an air of expectation, of waiting for something to happen. At night, however, it took on a peaceful quality, much like a child slowly settling into sleep.

From the evidence of litter left in the stands and the overflowing trash containers Dawn surmised that opening night had been a success. Brian would be pleased.

As she was digging her car keys out of her purse she spotted movement in the press box. A moment later whoever it was started down the long column of stairs, weighed down by an indistinguishable load. She started up the stairs to meet the figure and offer her assistance. By the time she recognized Brian it was too late to back down.

"You are indeed a jack-of-all-trades. Are you sure this is in your job description?" she asked, striving for a light tone as she took a portable speaker from his arms. "Is there any part of this operation you don't attend to personally?"

"I don't put ice packs on knees."

Was that meant as some form of criticism? Because she didn't want to have to consider that possibility, she fell in line beside Brian as they reached the ground level. "I hope we can continue to win," she offered. "That's one way of bringing in the paying customers."

"Is that what's on your mind? Money?"

"Money has been around a long time. It's a fact of

life. I don't know what it is with you. Sometimes I don't think I'll ever say the right thing around you."

He turned toward her. "I'm sorry if I've hurt your feelings, Dawn. But I have a great deal on my mind these days. I don't always take time to weigh the possible consequences of every word I utter before I open my mouth."

"I understand that," she responded. "All I'm asking for is some indication that I'm not the last person you want to be around."

Brian deposited his load on the ground and faced her again. "Did I ever say that? I swear you read things into our relationship that I never intended to put there."

"Do I?" Her voice took on a choked quality as she fought to sort out exactly what he was saying. "I—I can't forget how you treated me when we were dancing. You despised me."

"I don't like cheap tricks."

Dawn quivered under his brutal stare but refused to give way. "What cheap trick? You wanted me to play a public relations role, didn't you? You wanted me to flatter those men, to convince them that we all had the franchise's best interests at heart. I did that." She clenched her fists. "I danced and talked and listened until I thought I was going to lose my mind."

"You loved every minute of it," he pressed, giving her no quarter. "Do you think I'm blind? You didn't pull that dress out of a closet and throw it on in the dark. You knew darn well the impact you were making."

"Is that a crime!"

"It's a cheap trick." He leaned even closer, absorbing her with his presence. "You're not going to try to pretend there was no connection between what you wore the other night and the outfit you had on ten years ago, are you?"

Defeated, Dawn shook her head. "Was it so awful?" she whispered.

Instead of answering, he picked up the loudspeakers and headed toward his office. "Don't leave," he called back over his shoulder. "I'll be right back."

Every instinct tuned to emotional survival was warning Dawn to flee to the safety of her lonely house. But she stayed. Cruel as he could be, shattering as he was to her emotions, being near Brian was better than being away from him.

She didn't try to deny the leap her heart took when he reappeared. As he came to stand beside her, she resolved to ask no personal questions, nothing that might trigger his darker emotions. "Trouble with the speakers?" she asked.

"I'm going to have them replaced. The quality of sound isn't as good as it could be. Come with me. Since you're so interested in how this complex operates, I'll give you the guided tour."

"You don't have to," Dawn attempted nervously as his arm went easily around her waist. He pulled her tight against him but didn't glance in her direction.

It was as if she hadn't spoken. His attitude showed that he simply hadn't considered that she would object to what he was doing. Mutely she let him lead her onto the now-silent diamond. In a way she was grateful for his supporting arm. Her legs barely obeyed her command to walk and her body felt both feathery and inflamed. It was all she could do to keep her breath from coming in strangled gulps. It wasn't possible that a man's touch could instantly turn her into a warm and hungry woman, but it was happening.

Only a small percentage of what Brian was saying registered in her numb mind. He went on about the resodding needed in the infield, renting a roller to pack the base paths, hiring an electrician to update the lighting system, but if Dawn made any response to his comments, she was unaware of it. It was only when he asked her if she knew of any graphic artist who might work on a logo for Verdue Field that she focused on the conversation. Her answer, she was afraid, was unsatisfactory.

"I'd like to work with a woman," he was saying. "My idea may be more masculine than it should be. I want Verdue Field to appeal to both sexes and all ages."

"That's refreshing to hear," she said, stumbling into the conversation before thinking. "There are still men who don't believe women can function as professionals."

"Professionals, yes. On a personal level it can be another matter."

"We've come back to that, have we?" Dawn was aware of the almost sad tone in her voice, but her emotions were wild, beyond her control. "Why won't you admit it? You don't have anything good to say about women."

Brian's hand tightened around her waist, bringing an end to their walk. "You haven't been through the past few years with me. Until you know what it's like to have to fight for the right to your son, you'll have no idea."

"She's only one woman," Dawn ventured, shrinking beneath the knotted strength in his arm. "It shouldn't make you hate all women."

"I never said it did. You're the one who's using that word."

"How can I help it?" she moaned. "I feel your loathing every time I'm around you."

"Loathing?" Brian's laugh was a harsh slap to her emotions. "Don't disillusion yourself. I assure you, my feelings toward you are much more neutral."

Could she believe that? Did she want to? Dawn asked herself. She tried to free herself by placing her hands on Brian's chest and pushing. Instead of freeing her, he gripped her wrists in steel fingers and held her helpless before him. "Love is an emotion I have no intention of punishing myself with again. And your little game of wearing white isn't going to work. That might have accomplished its goal a few years ago, but no longer." His eyes shot searing daggers deep inside her.

"Thank you for spelling it out. For your information, it echoes my sentiments exactly." Her heart was saying the opposite. "Let me go! I'll never bother you again."

Suddenly his lips were on hers, lips that sought to control, to overwhelm. She couldn't believe he hadn't planned this to prove his mastery over her. Dawn fought their impact on her senses as a drowning man fights the tide. If she gave in now to her heart, she would be lost. She needed no one to tell her that.

But there was no fighting the swell of emotion surging through her. Brian may be punishing her, but punishment from him was far better than anything she'd experienced from another man. It taught her fully what it meant to be a woman, to realize that she'd been born to love a man—this man.

"Stop, please. What are you doing?" she whimpered when he gave her time to breathe.

"Don't talk" was all he said. He effectively stopped her by again pressing his lips against hers in a commanding move. Dawn melted against him, a helpless captive. No matter that he had no feelings for her—that heart-wrenching reality belonged to a lifetime of tears—this moment was for gathering enough memories to make it through the lonely years.

She felt her body reaching out for him and knew no shame as her breasts were crushed against his chest. His hands locked around her back and held her tight against him. His kiss was a challenge, one she knew she would never beat. He was testing her strength and asking for proof that his neutrality was a twin to her own emotions.

Dawn failed the test completely. She heard the moan escape from her lips and was grateful for the arms that kept her from collapsing. Her own arms developed a will of their own. She placed them around his neck and lifted herself onto her toes in order to secure her hold on him. It didn't matter that he knew what she was feeling. She wanted him.

Only the night creatures flying around the stadium lights knew how long the two humans remained locked in each other's arms. What those creatures saw was a woman with tears in her heart, looking desperately into the granite face of a man who seemed to find it hard to control his breathing.

"Neutral feelings," he said.

And she trembled.

Chapter Eight

Dawn glanced at her bedroom clock, but even the relentless march of the minute hand wasn't enough to make her attend to her packing.

Why did Brian have to be going along on this road trip? Surely he had enough to do at Verdue Field, she thought. He certainly didn't have to join the team during the swing north that would take five days and four games. But Brian had announced that he wanted to take a look at other field operations, talk to the managers there, and perhaps incorporate some of their ideas into Verdue Field.

But they'd all be checking into the same motel, and Dawn was, quite frankly, terrified that she would be unable to survive the close contact with her sanity intact.

She stared at the clothes hanging in her closet, her hand straying over the white dress. No. She wouldn't take it. In fact, she couldn't imagine herself ever wearing it again. Then why didn't she give it away?

Because it still wore the imprint of Brian's arms around her as they danced. The dress was a memory, she realized, Dawn's one remaining link with a perfect evening that had somehow gone all wrong.

"Why are you doing this to me?" she moaned. But for the life of her she didn't know whether she was talking to herself or Brian. As if it hadn't been clear enough the night of the cocktail party, he'd spelled out his position the other night under the lights of Verdue Field. His feelings toward her were neutral. And the tone of his voice, his masterful kiss, only served to reinforce his edict. He must have known that she'd lost all will to oppose him. If he'd wanted to make love to her on the rich grass, she would have offered no resistance. In fact, her body had been willing, eager even, to respond fully to his.

But he'd stopped with that punishing kiss. And in the week since then he hadn't said a single word to her. Yes, he was busy implementing the improvements he'd talked about with her, and she'd seen Tad with him, but did he have to act as if she didn't exist?

Oh, what do I care, she thought, slamming a pair of jeans into her suitcase. *It's best this way. He doesn't have any feelings for me, for any woman. He's really being kind—at least in the long run.* The old saying "absence makes the heart grow fonder" was something Dawn wasn't convinced of. Hadn't she gradually gotten over Brian the first time during those ten years of separation?

It could happen again. It had to if she was going to retain her sanity.

Because her whirling thoughts were giving her a headache, Dawn grabbed the phone to tell her mother where she'd be and ask her to water the half dozen plants she was trying to grow in her house. She didn't reach her mother at home, but finally ran her down at Peter's office. Crystal explained that the political campaign was now in high gear and she was devoting a lot of time to doing research on the county's financial picture.

"Are you driving up?" Crystal asked. "Maybe you'll have time to do some sight-seeing while you're there."

Dawn explained that the team, manager, and trainer were expected to ride together in the chartered bus. "It's going to be interesting," she admitted. "I've never been on an eight-hour trip with a bus full of bored, wisecracking young men. My ears will probably be pretty red by the end of this. Except for baseball, they only have one other thing on their minds." She laughed. "I'm not sure whether women or baseball comes first."

"What about Brian? I hope he'll be going."

"Why?" she had to ask.

Crystal laughed. "Just motherly concern, dear. I like that man. He's making things happen in his life. I believe that's the only kind of man who'd ever satisfy you. After all, you've always taken control of your life. You need someone who can complement you."

"Brian isn't interested in a romance, Mom," Dawn said through suddenly numb lips. She wasn't a psychiatrist, but she felt she knew what had happened to the carefree football hero. "I think he invested a great deal of himself in his marriage. When it didn't work out, he decided he'd learned his lesson. The only person he cares about is his son."

Crystal protested. "I can't believe that. When he talked to me the other night, I got the distinct impression that he was interested in meeting me and not just making conversation. I'd like to think it was my sparkling wit, but I think you were the link.''

''You don't know him the way I do'' was all Dawn could say. ''And in answer to your question, he's going to the games. But he's taking his own car. He said he's going to be doing a lot of running around. Look, I'm really going to be late if I don't get moving. Give my love to Peter.''

And yet despite her words, Dawn sat staring at the telephone instead of returning to her packing. Her mother had had her father for all those years. Their marriage had been a happy one that fulfilled the needs of both of them. Even as a widow her mother wasn't being shut away from an adult relationship. Dawn wouldn't be surprised to see her mother remarry. Why was it possible for her mother to find two loving men in her life when all Dawn had done was spend her adult life trapped in an unattainable dream?

She was afraid she knew why she hadn't married. Her heart, the secret inner recesses of her heart, hadn't forgotten Brian. She was still sealed to him, still possessed by him as she'd been when she was really too young to know what love was all about.

Had she learned anything in all those years? Or was she still trapped emotionally in an adolescent love? The only thing Dawn knew was that she had to break Brian's hold on her. He felt nothing for her. Her only chance for any kind of life led in severing the ties that had existed for ten years.

And in the process she was determined to keep her feelings from Brian. If nothing else, Dawn had her pride. She wasn't going to let anyone, especially Brian, know that she had so little control over her feelings, that she was the prisoner of a hopeless, one-sided love.

Dawn ran a hand over her eyes and stared resolutely at her suitcase. It was filled with jeans and loose-fitting baseball jerseys, which stood in contrast to the high-cut bikini panties and lace-trimmed bras. Underneath she was deeply feminine, but on the surface she was disgustingly practical. Feeling decidedly bored with her workaday attire, she grabbed a berry-colored ruffled-neck lightweight sweater and button-front matching skirt and folded them on top of the suitcase. Now she was ready to turn into a woman on a cool northern evening if the occasion arose.

Was that what women wore to singles' clubs? She'd never been to one, so she didn't know, but in her present mood any action, no matter how reckless, was preferable to moping around the way she was doing.

The team's luggage had been packed into the bus's belly when Dawn arrived. She'd already inventoried the first aid kit so had little to do except take note of where her suitcase landed and then watch the high jinks of the young men as they discussed the possibilities for one-night stands. Some of them, Big Bob in particular, were crude in their assessment of the women who came to games and hung around the dugouts, hoping to catch a male eye. There weren't many women who made such blatant displays of themselves, but Dawn accepted that fact of life. The ballplayers had been uprooted from their hometowns. Despite being surrounded by their teammates, they had to be lonely for feminine companionship. It was natural that women with hot romance on their minds would be aware of that and take advantage of it.

Not that the women were the aggressors all the time. From the way some of the young men acted, it was clear that both sides knew how the game was played. It made Dawn feel part of another generation.

Coach Weatherby passed on the news that Brian had already left and would meet the team when they arrived in Seattle. "That's one man with a lot on his mind," the manager observed. "He said his lawyer has been working to set the date for a custody hearing. Brian's hinging a lot on that. It's plain he wants that boy in the worst way. I don't know what he's so uptight about. He's a damn good father."

"But a lot of judges still believe children belong with their mothers. I'm sure Brian's aware of that." Despite her resolve to dismiss Brian from her thoughts, Dawn couldn't pretend she couldn't relate to what Brian was going through, and sympathize.

The trip north would always stand out in Dawn's mind as one of the most uncomfortable of her life. The bus the team had leased for the year had obviously been built with economy and not comfort in mind. If the seats had any padding in them, it was too scant to be noticed. The shocks must have seen fifty thousand more miles than they were designed for. Ventilation was poor. At first the young men joked about girlie magazines, but eventually they fell silent, some of them trying to nap with their heads resting on hard seat backs. Dawn squirmed and twisted in the seat she shared with Coach Weatherby. She tried to doze, but the wiry manager had fallen asleep and was snoring through his open mouth. To make matters worse, his head found her shoulder, and she spent hours with its weight adding to her discomfort. The sun had set when the bus finally passed the city limits. A collective sigh went up, and Weatherby snorted and sat upright. He patted Dawn's aching shoulder. "Young lady, I'm going to buy you the tallest, fruitiest drink we can find. One with a healthy shot of booze in it."

Dawn didn't object. She hadn't eaten since breakfast, as the sandwiches passed around for lunch on the bus were gone before they reached her. She felt hot and sticky, her head filled with cobwebs. At the moment she wanted nothing more than to sit in air-conditioned comfort and unwind over the fruity drink the manager had tempted her with.

Settling into the small motel room set aside for the one female traveling with the team took only a few minutes. Dawn freshened up by washing her face and applying fresh lipstick. She changed into the skirt and sweater and slipped her feet into a pair of sandals.

Coach Weatherby whistled appreciatively when she joined him in the lobby. "Now I really am glad I asked you out instead of one of those characters. I swear, they eat more than it's healthy for anyone. I'd probably have to pick up the tab to boot. I hope you're ready to forget that we're baby-sitting those overgrown kids."

Dawn linked her arm through the manager's and gave a little skip. It felt good to have a man for a friend, one she could be comfortable around because nothing of a sexual nature surfaced. After they'd walked across the street from the motel to the dimly lit tropical-style cocktail lounge, Dawn nodded agreement to the pineapple-flavored drink Coach Weatherby offered and took a sip. "If I fall asleep here, don't wake me." She moaned in contentment.

"You better get to sleep early. I'm calling a morning practice to get ready for the game. These kids are acting like they've been let out of school. I plan on dashing any idea they have that this is a vacation. Besides, I suspect Brian is going to want to meet with me in the afternoon."

"Where is he? Is he checked into the motel?" Dawn hadn't wanted to ask at the office, but it seemed like an innocent enough question now.

"Yep. His room is just around the corner from yours. Only other single room on the second floor. I don't know how much we'll see of him. He had an agenda lined up for himself that's going to run him ragged. But that's his job, and I guess he knows what he's doing."

Dawn let her mind drift as Coach Weatherby launched into a monologue of all the motels he'd been to over the course of his coaching career. She didn't want to think about Brian, but her mind refused to turn in any other direction. Her mind's eye saw him bent over to listen to the little boy standing by his side. Strange. She'd thought she'd be more likely to remember their night of dancing, but maybe the other picture was more representative of the real Brian. Coach Weatherby was right. Brian was a good father.

A good father, a competent businessman, someone who thrived on challenge.

Dawn shook her head to shake off the cobwebs in her mind. She was on track about much of her abortive relationship with Brian, but up until this moment she'd been wrong about one fundamental.

She wasn't in love with memories. She was in fact

in love with the man of today. It wasn't a matter of clinging to her youth and a girl's notions of what her heart's hero should be. That had been buried where it belonged. Her feelings for Brian this evening had nothing to do with what they'd been ten years ago. The football hero had turned into a man she couldn't help but respect—and love. He'd put his college degree to good use and was equal to the challenge of his demanding job. But he was more than a man with the ability to turn ideas into action.

He was a deeply caring human being, at least when it came to his son.

Unfortunately, to her grief, that capacity for caring didn't extend to her.

Again Dawn gave herself a mental shake. What she thought of Brian wasn't helping her cope with reality. Hadn't she given herself a stern talking-to? She was going to get over her feelings for Brian. She had to if she was going to go on with the act of living.

"Speaking of the devil!" Coach Weatherby said suddenly. "Here comes the workaholic himself."

Dawn looked up to trace the movement of the man she loved as he threaded his way around the intimate tables and finally came to stand next to them. "I thought I'd find you here," he was saying to the manager. "If there's one man who knows where to go to relax, it's you. Do you mind if I join you?" He pulled out a chair without waiting for a response. A cold shock of realization shot through Dawn as she saw how he was favoring his right knee. Instead of folding it under the table, he kept it stretched out to one side. He rubbed it absently as he inquired about the bus ride.

"Old war wound kicking up again?" Coach Weatherby observed.

Brian shrugged it off. "That knee's never been right. Surgery helped, but not enough."

"Have you seen a doctor lately?" Dawn asked. She didn't like the way his lips were set in a hard line. As a nurse she knew what pain on a man's face looked like.

"Later. But not now."

"Why not?" she pressed. "I've seen you favoring it before. It isn't getting any better."

"I have my reasons" was all he said. His eyes were a shield holding her away from him.

Dawn didn't attempt to enter the conversation. She had all she could do to fight off the effect of having him near. There'd been times when she was physically attracted to Jim, but it had never been anything like this. Every nerve ending in her body ached for Brian's touch. Her emotions had turned traitor, drawing her relentlessly into bondage. Her fingers pulled with the need to make contact with the dark hairs resting on his muscled forearm. What would it do to her senses if he placed his fingers on the hollow of her throat and traced a line down to her breasts?

She took a deep gasping breath and drew her body firmly upright. No! She couldn't dare think about that! She'd be reaching for the buttons of his shirt in a minute if she didn't get control of herself.

"I have some heat treatment that might help your knee," she blurted in a desperate attempt to give her mind something else to focus on.

"Were we talking about my knee?" He turned on her. "Coach, I don't know how much this young woman has had to drink, but it's gone to her cheeks. She's glowing like an embarrassed schoolgirl."

Brian's taunt was her undoing. Dawn was helpless to fight the deep flush that coursed through her and turned her cheeks to burning coals. "I—I missed out on lunch," she stammered. "That's all it is."

"Then eat. I swear." He shook his head like a long-suffering parent faced with an unreasoning child. "You'd think we had enough to do keeping these young jocks from putting the entire female population of this city to flight. Now we have to wet-nurse a nurse. Don't you know your blood sugar level hits rock bottom after too many hours of no nourishment?"

That isn't the kind of nourishment that's bothering me, Dawn thought, but of course she'd rather die than admit it. Gratefully she accepted the suggestion that they check out the reputation of the adjoining restaurant. As she was eating the small salad that came before the main course, she realized Brian was right. "You should have been a doctor," she observed, grateful that she was now more in control of her senses. "Food is exactly what I needed."

"Oh? Most women need more than food to sustain them."

Was he goading her? Dawn cringed under the unexpected comment and concentrated on her plate. "At the moment that's all that concerns me," she said, taking a healthy bite to reinforce her statement.

"I find that hard to believe. I understand that most women's appetites take many forms and directions."

"Is that a criticism of women?" she asked, her nerves taut.

"It's a statement based on personal experience. Let's just say that some perverse appetites can be quite effective in destroying certain relationships. Eat up, Miss Morrell. I certainly don't intend to ruin my appetite by dredging up my past."

True to his word, Brian launched into an overview of what he'd learned by meeting with another general manager earlier in the day. He'd learned that the problems he was encountering at Verdue Field appeared to be universal. "It appears that all manner of organizations look at a baseball franchise as a profitable venture. I'm not the only one who receives numerous requests from nonprofit groups for financial support. It's simply a matter of picking and choosing which ones I'm going to be able to help. Because this organization is involved in sports, I'm going to limit myself to assisting youth sports activities for the most part. I did learn of some ways to make Verdue Field accessible to American Legion and college teams without it hurting us."

Dawn kept her eyes on Brian during his speech, hoping that he read her expression as that of simply attentiveness. She could only pray that he knew nothing of her underlying feelings. Whenever she felt her control slip, she let her eyes stray to the other diners, the decorations, the movements of waitresses, anything for distraction.

"Am I boring you?" she finally heard Brian say.

"Oh, no." Quickly she pasted a smile on her face. "But until you've spent eight hours on a bus with someone snoring in your ear, you don't know what a long day is. Inactivity can be exhausting. I'm afraid eating may be the last thing I do today."

"Pity. I was going to take you on a tour."

No! She'd never survive being alone in a car with Brian! "I'll have to take a rain check on that," she replied. "At this point sleep is the only thing I'm interested in."

If Brian's look was more piercing than before, Dawn managed to shrug off a desire to ponder the reason. She wasn't making up an excuse. With her stomach taken care of, she had to admit that the heavy feeling in her arms and legs would only be relieved by a night spent in bed. As soon as their bill had been taken care of, Dawn said her good-byes and walked back across the street to the motel. She noted the steam rising from the swimming pool in front and made a mental note to try it out in the morning.

Because she had doubts that she could be assured of privacy, she'd brought along a dorm shirt with a shirttail bottom for sleeping in. It fit loosely over her body, the side slit revealing a whisper of panty. She pulled back the covers and slipped into bed. But the sleep she'd expected wouldn't come. A half hour later she gave in, sat up, and opened a paperback to a plot she couldn't describe if her life depended on it. She was trying to recall what a character by the name of Bear had to do with a story about an island resort when she heard the knock at the door.

"Dawn? You still awake?"

She jumped at the sound of the one voice capable of undoing all her newly regained self-control and slipped out of bed. Reluctantly she opened the door and peered out at Brian. "Did you get lost? Weatherby said your room was down the hall."

"I know where my room is." Brian wiped a hand across his face before continuing. "Don't mind me. In the mood I'm in, I probably shouldn't be talking to anyone."

"Then why are you?"

"You said something about treatment for a knee?"

Dawn's heart went out to Brian. The tight look on his face had increased and he was standing with his weight on his good leg. "Of course." She took his hand and pulled him into the room. It no longer mattered that this was the man who could bring her to the brink of emotional disaster simply by coming into sight. Dawn Morrell was a nurse. And at that moment the nurse in her switched into high gear.

She unceremoniously commanded Brian to remove his slacks and then ordered him to sit on the bed with his legs stretched out in front of him. Dawn sat next to him and ran her fingers along his knee until he sucked in his breath sharply. "That's the spot," he said lightly, but Dawn could tell what the comment was costing him in self-control.

"What happened?" she asked as she traced the outline of his surgical scar.

"I got hit in a game."

"I could figure that out. I read the newspaper account," she said in the tone she used with stubborn patients. "I'm talking about the surgery. What did they have to do?"

"I don't recall all the technical aspects, but I was most impressed by the sight of my dislocated kneecap. I have to admit I lost a fair amount of composure over that."

"What else?" Brian was impossible! What was it

about men that made them feel they were trading in their masculinity to admit to injury?

"Torn ligaments and cartilage. Some thigh muscle went down for the count too. The surgeon made things so I could walk again, but he said if I didn't want to risk winding up a cripple, I had to stop being a tackling dummy for some two-hundred-fifty-pound lineman."

"Has it been bothering you long? You haven't been putting up with this for years, have you?" she asked as she reached for a tube of liniment she'd gotten from a valley doctor for just such occasions.

"Not long. A few weeks. Look, do I have to give you the whole history? You said something about a heat treatment."

"I could put a Band-Aid on it. A big one so you can brag to all your friends." She turned serious. "I swear, I don't understand you. Don't you know you're playing with fire? You already have a knee that's been subjected to a lot of punishment. If it's started to bother you again, it's not going to go away simply because I rub a little cream over it. You really should see a doctor. The one who gave me this is the one I'd recommend."

"Spare me the lecture." Brian's muscles tensed as her fingers came in contact with a sensitive area. "I intend on going in for whatever repair it needs, but not now."

"Why not? Surely you're not so indispensable to the organization that you can't attend to something as essential as your personal health. Even the president takes time for a physical."

"It has nothing to do with my job," Brian said through tight lips. "Look, do you have to do that? I have other reasons for not wanting to be laid up right now.''

''And you're not going to tell me. Is that it?'' Another time his closemouthed attitude would have meant emotional ruin, but because she was functioning as a professional, she was able to be objective about such things. ''Don't tell me. The macho male has a certain image to maintain.''

''If that's what you want to believe, who am I to discourage you? That's better.'' He sighed. ''I can feel the heat deep in my knee.''

Dawn continued her gentle massage, relieved to see the tension go out of Brian's body. Slowly he lay back on the bed and lifted an arm to cover his eyes. Dawn bent over him, her fingers light on the obviously swollen joint. She felt pain leave her own body as his breathing lengthened and became shallow. How long she sat ministering to him she had no idea. There was no denying she could be content to spend the rest of the night—the rest of her life—sitting on the same bed with Brian Riegel.

She studied him, secure in the knowledge that he couldn't know that her eyes were absorbing him and committing him to memory. His hair grew thick and unruly, a cowlick at his forehead creating an interesting hairline. Upon close inspection she could make out a few stray gray hairs. It made him even more human in her eyes. Like everyone else, Brian wasn't immune to the maturing process. It bothered her somewhat to realize he was young for gray hairs. He refused to discuss his marriage and its breakdown, but there was no hiding its effect on him.

The chest hairs visible under his shirt crawled up to

the base of his throat. If they hadn't been so fair, they might have given him a slightly bearlike look. But they were fine, like spun silk. What would they feel like to her sensitive fingers?

Brian looked out from under cover of his arm. "I'm not keeping you up, am I?"

"Oh, no. I guess I was too tired to sleep." She nodded toward the book on the nightstand, quickly collecting her thoughts enough to enable her to carry on a conversation. "I was trying to read. That usually relaxes me."

"Good book?"

"I can't seem to concentrate on the plot. Maybe it's a sign of old age. I hope I'm not getting senile." The joke was a ploy to keep him from thinking that he might be responsible for her distracted state.

"You don't look old."

A chill shot through Dawn. How closely was he watching her these days? Was she measuring up? she wanted to know. "I appreciate the comment. But I've aged since—since the last time we had anything to do with each other."

Brian continued to stare at her. "We seem to keep coming back to that, don't we. It was a long time ago, Dawn."

"I know. You've made it clear that you have no interest in discussing the past." Her hands were held in a tight knot on her lap as she struggled with self-control. "I'm trying to respect that. I didn't mean to let it slip out like that. I assure you, it won't happen again."

"Why do you think I would want to pretend it never happened?"

"Do you have to ask? I haven't forgotten your re-action to my white dress. That's all the lesson I need, thank you."

"Can you blame me? Truthfully, I wasn't prepared for my reaction." He sat up and took her hands, slowly uncurling the taut fingers. "It was like going back in time ten years."

"Is that so terrible?" Her self-control was slipping. She wasn't sure she still had the strength to hold on to it.

"For me it was. Dawn, I've been going through a rocky period in my life. I don't want, or need, any complications."

"Then I suggest you leave." She wanted that. Didn't she? "I'm not wearing white, but I don't think it takes a dress to trigger the past."

"No. It doesn't." Brian sighed. His eyes took on a reflective quality. "I felt like I'd been hit by a line drive when you walked in that night. I don't think anyone or anything has ever affected me the way you did. I didn't believe I still possessed whatever it takes to respond in that fashion."

Having him so close, being so deeply tuned to his masculinity, stripped Dawn of her defenses. She was still dimly aware that the past was a closed book with him. But it was impossible to adhere to the ground rules he'd set up as long as he insisted on staying so close to her, his long naked legs giving out the mes-sage of his sensuality. Dawn knew there was no future with Brian for her. What did it matter if she destroyed the slim web still holding them together? At least, maybe, she'd have the answer to the question that haunted her for so many years.

"That night, ten years ago. Did you want me?"

He blinked, proof, she realized, that he hadn't expected the question. But instead of pulling away, he sat up and reached out to take a handful of ivory hair in his fingers. "Oh, my little angel. You have no idea how much I wanted you."

Dawn shuddered, joy erasing the ability to feel fear. She was reckless with relief. He had wanted her! In all those years she'd never been sure.

"Then, why didn't you make love to me?"

A groan escaped his lips and he pulled her next to him on the bed, her bare legs brushing against his own. "I didn't know you."

"I knew you," she blurted. "Brian, I watched your every move for a year before that party. I don't think I really looked at another boy in all that time. I read everything the paper wrote about you. Remember that last awards ceremony in high school? When I saw you walk onto the stage to receive your trophies, I felt as if I were by your side. I went home and cried because your success had become mine."

"You were quite the star-struck kid, weren't you?"

She had to laugh because Brian had read her so well. "Oh, yes." Her tentative fingers found the soft hairs on his chest and began to commit them to memory. She felt shy about what she was doing and yet her need was the greater emotion. "You have no idea how many—love letters I wrote to you. Fortunately, I burned them before I could give in to the impulse to send them."

"Why?" They were sitting so close that she could feel his breath on her cheek.

"Can't you guess?" This time her laugh was a little

forced. She was being asked to bare her soul, to reveal for the first time the young dreams she'd kept buried inside all these years. "My girl friends had crushes on rock stars, actors. Not me. I set my sights much closer to home. That thought terrified me. I was better off dreaming my hopeless dreams."

"I wouldn't have scorned you," he whispered, his lips a scant inch away. "But maybe you're right. I don't think you would have liked who I was in those days."

"I can't believe that."

"Believe it." He stopped her by placing his fingers over her lips. "I hope you can understand and not judge me too harshly. But I was pretty impressionable myself. All that attention went to my head. I had an ego that wouldn't stop. I tried to tell myself that I put on my pants one leg at a time just like everyone else, but I'm not sure I really believed that. Dawn, I had girls calling the house all hours of the day and night. Some of them made suggestions that even embarrassed me. It sounds conceited, I'm afraid, but I could have had my pick in those days."

"Did you?" she asked from under the living gag that was his hand.

"That, my young lady, is better left unsaid. Let's just say that I didn't lack for attention." A cloud passed over his features. "But it wasn't what I wanted."

"You didn't want all those girls chasing after you?"

"They weren't interested in me," he explained, his fingers back to caressing her hair. "They were attracted by the public figure the press made me out to be. I can admit that now. Thanks to the local paper and what was being said at school, I was being transformed into someone even I didn't know." He groaned. "I'd read about how the school's hopes for a state championship were resting on my shoulders and think, God, how did this happen to me? What I'm trying to say is that all the time I was soaking up this attention I was also scared."

"I never knew."

"I never told anyone. Not even my family. Fear isn't something for the big campus hero to admit, is it?"

"I wouldn't have told anyone," she whispered, aching with understanding for what Brian had had to endure alone. He'd had a terrible responsibility placed on his shoulders.

"But I didn't know that," he whispered back. "Dawn, I didn't know you. You were a white-haired girl who stood out only because of that hair. It wasn't until that night at my house that you became a flesh and blood woman. Oh, God, did you! I've never felt anything the way I did when I saw you standing there. And when I took you in my arms—" He left the rest unsaid.

"I was so nervous, I almost didn't come—" she started, but he stopped her with a kiss.

"You did. That's all that matters." They were no longer sitting apart from each other. Brian took her in his arms, his fingers finding the flesh at the top of her neck. She responded completely to the kiss that sealed them together.

There was no need for further talk then. Dawn was supremely content to remain in the circle of his arms, committing this man to memory, feeling her heart swell with a happiness she didn't know possible.

She could feel his warm healthy body next to hers and realized that her own body was responding as a woman responds to a man. Her breath came quicker and her nerve endings seemed capable of registering a sensuality she'd never dreamed possible. Her head filled with the message of his kiss, of his maleness, as she pressed her breasts against his chest.

Finally, though, the awkwardness of their position drew them momentarily apart. When she'd been freed of him enough to be permitted thought, Dawn came back to the question that had triggered this moment. "Brian, please, I have to know," she managed, despite the restless surging of emotions she had only momentary control over. "You must have known I was ready to give myself to you that night. I wanted you so much. Nothing else mattered. Why didn't you make love to me? Was it really because you didn't know me?"

For answer he gave a slight shake of his head. "That wasn't all of it," he explained. "But it was a start. It was the only explanation I had. Dawn, you were different from the other girls. I don't know why or how, but you were. I felt it the moment I looked into your eyes. If I'd made love to you, I was afraid you'd be like the others. I wanted what we were experiencing to remain special."

"But you never got in touch with me again." That was what was so hard to say.

"I injured my knee the next week." His voice was flat, dead. "For a long time I couldn't think of anything except my shattered dreams. God, I was bitter. I didn't want to be around people. I didn't want people pointing and saying 'remember when.' That's why I changed colleges. I couldn't stand being reminded that I was no longer living up to everyone's expectations. And you?" He stifled a sound that sounded a little like the moan of a wounded animal. "Dawn, I couldn't even think of you without feeling like I was going out of my mind. I kept thinking—I thought you wouldn't want a man with a scarred-up knee, one who had no idea what he was going to do with the rest of his life. I was no longer what brought you to me."

Dawn was silent. She would like to be able to deny his statement, but in her heart of hearts maybe she couldn't. Back then she was a babe in the world of love. Her emotions were triggered by a flash of strength on a football field and a self-confident man lifting a trophy over his head while a whole school applauded. That's what had attracted her to him in those days. She didn't know what might have happened to her feelings had she seen the end to the spell she'd woven around Brian Riegel.

But that was the past. Tonight was for what they'd become.

As before, she traced the outline of Brian's surgical scar. "It gives you character," she acknowledged softly. "No one's perfect."

Brian lifted her fingers off his knee and brought them to his lips. "Dreams of perfection are for children," he said. "We have to live in the real world."

"And what is the real world?" Did he know that in one way she was still that girl from the past? One word from him and she would spend the night in his arms.

"No serious questions, Dawn. It's too late for that."

Brian taught her what he meant. She sat unmoving as he placed his hands on her throat and brushed his way around to the outline of her collarbone. Inside she was being ignited into a thousand flames, but somehow she willed herself to remain still. This moment was one she'd given up dreaming would ever happen. Although it took the utmost in self-control, she was determined to experience it to the fullest. A soft sigh escaped her lips as his exploring fingers found the soft swell of her breasts. He met her mouth with lips that knew how to trigger the fullest emotion of a woman. The inner flame expanded, coursing through her limbs until she wondered if she was on the verge of passing out. But the risk was worth taking. Ecstasy was the goal her body craved—demanded even.

When she doubted her ability to maintain her fragile grip on self-control, Brian lifted the nightshirt over her head. She sat exposed before him, trembling like a young girl on her first date. Did he approve of what he saw? Steady exercise kept her physically trim, but her breasts were small and her hipbones more prominent than she wanted. Her flesh burned with a fire she believed there was no hiding.

With fingers that were strangely devoid of muscle, she managed to unfasten the buttons of his shirt and finally saw the rest of the chest that so fascinated her. She played with the fine hairs, wondering at the miracle that had brought her to this moment. What did it matter that there'd been other women before? They were in each other's arms. For a few hours at least they could forget everything except satisfying the needs of two hungry bodies.

Whatever happened during the rest of her life, she had tonight.

Brian's lips against hers, the sealing of two mouths, cut off all thought. Dawn offered no resistance as he stretched her along the length of the bed. *You know me. Now you know me,* played through her like a beloved melody.

It was a long time before the pinnacle was reached. Brian taught her things about her body that she'd never before been aware of. With his guidance she learned that she was capable of a deeper swell of emotion than she'd dreamed possible. He brought her to the brink of tears and beyond, tears born of love, wonder, and fulfillment. When at last he drew a sheet over them, she was ready. As a woman she'd known what lovemaking was, but as a woman in Brian Riegel's arms she was taken beyond everything she'd dreamed possible.

Brian didn't go to his room that night.

Chapter Nine

Dawn was a long time leaving the cocoon she'd become encased in sometime during the night. Her flesh still registered the existence of the man who'd slept with her. Her heart was still full of wonder at the fulfillment of all her dreams. Somewhere beyond her closed lids was a world to be faced, problems that were part of living. But first she would savor and cling to what had happened.

There'd been no words of love from Brian, but Dawn refused to dwell on that. She'd been made love to. That was all the woman in her needed for now. No ballplayer swinging at a home run pitch could possibly feel more satisfied than she did at this moment. A grand slam. Was that what last night was, a grand slam home run?

Finally, though, the light coming through the motel window stabbed its way through her thoughts and brought her reluctantly to face the day.

Brian was gone.

Dawn sat up and let the sheet slide off her nude body. She turned toward the bathroom, hoping he was in there, but there was no sound of running water to disturb the silence. She stood up and walked to the front door, feeling the air on her flesh. It was locked; she was sure they hadn't bothered to lock it last night. It wasn't until she'd turned back toward the room that she saw the note written on motel stationery resting on the nightstand.

"After my surgery, the doctor told me to take life one day at a time. That's what we have to do. Take what we have one day at a time."

Tears she had only minimum understanding of stung Dawn's eyes and sent her stumbling for the shower. What did he mean? Was he asking for a day-by-day existence? At dinner last night she'd tried to resign herself to the fact that what she felt for Brian was destined to remain a one-sided love. But that was before they'd talked honestly about what had happened ten years ago. Before they had made love.

Dawn couldn't forget that Brian had once had a wife and because of things that happened in that marriage he'd become wary and distrustful of women. His feelings weren't going to change overnight—even with her. Was that it? Did his reference to one day at a time mean he was testing his emotions in regard to her, not sure what was going to develop?

Or did he mean he was only interested in a physical relationship?

It couldn't be like that for her. Dawn loved Brian with a love that had matured and become full grown over the test of time. There was no way her heart would be satisfied with nights together and days apart and no commitment from him.

Dawn was grateful for the day's activities, which took her away from her thoughts and gave her practi-

cal matters to concern herself with. She joined the
team in the motel swimming pool for an early dip and
then had breakfast with Coach Weatherby. Brian
didn't appear, but the manager explained that Brian
had told him he had meetings for most of the day. It
hurt to realize that he hadn't told her of his plans, but
there wasn't anything she could do about that.

Dawn was frankly disappointed with Colver Field.
She'd expected a more impressive stadium, but apparently the farm team here didn't enjoy the popularity
those playing at Verdue Field did already. Her impression appeared to be shared by the team as they trotted
onto the uneven infield for practice. They continued
to grumble until the manager threatened them with a
number of laps around the outfield unless they attended to business. Dawn had no real duties during
the morning workout, but because she had no trans-
portation in the city and was hesitant to spend money
on sight-seeing, she stayed during the two-hour ses-
sion. She kept hoping Brian would appear, but by the
time the team broke for lunch there was no sign of the
general manager.

Coach Weatherby offered to see if they could rent a
car and take in the city, but Dawn declined. She simply told him that last night hadn't resulted in the sleep
she needed following the long bus trip. "I think I'll
just lie out by the pool. Maybe I'll take a short nap."

"If you get sunburned, I know a nurse who can fix
you up," he teased.

Dawn settled for a salad in the adjacent restaurant
and then changed into a kelly-green low-backed bathing suit. She sat in one of the lawn chairs at the pool's
edge and once again tried to pick up the plot of the book

she'd been reading last night. Before long the words blurred and her head rolled to one side. The few vacationers around the pool left her to doze undisturbed.

Dawn had been asleep for over an hour when she felt someone shaking her shoulders. "You're going to wind up looking like a lobster. It's a good thing you're already tanned, or you'd really be in trouble."

Dawn squinted up into the sunlight. She couldn't make out the features of the man standing above her, but her heart had already memorized his voice. "What time is it?" she asked sleepily.

"Time for bathing beauties to jump into the pool and cool off. You have a decided burn there." Brian ran his fingers along the base of her throat and showed her the glistening tips. "I understand it's polite to say that women only glow, but that's about the healthiest glow I've ever seen."

Dawn scrambled off her chair. Now that she was awake she realized how hot and uncomfortable she felt. Brian's suggestion of a cool dip sounded exactly like what the doctor ordered. Without speaking she walked to the side of the pool and dove in. A moment later she surfaced, gasping at the sudden temperature change. "I'm cold!" she spluttered. "Why didn't you tell me it was freezing in here?"

"I don't recall you asking." Brian slipped out of the terry cloth wrap he was wearing and joined her in the pool. For several minutes they swam together silently. Dawn gave herself a goal of twenty laps, switching from crawl to backstroke and then to sidestroke, concentrating on her form and breathing. Brian kept her pace, although it was obvious that he was the faster swimmer.

Finally, Dawn swam to the shallow end and stood up, shaking back her wet hair. "I needed that. I didn't realize I was so tired out. A little nap and some exercise and I'm ready for the rest of the day."

"Didn't you get enough sleep last night?" If Brian was teasing, he didn't let it show in his voice.

Dawn blushed. They couldn't be assured of privacy, so she attempted to keep the conversation neutral, at least on the surface. "I think you know the answer to that. I found your note."

Brian nodded but said nothing. Instead, he started to tell her about his day's activities. As he spoke Dawn felt rather like a secretary being caught up on her boss's schedule. There was nothing personal in his speech, and when his leg brushed against hers in the water, she was sure it was accidental. "I hope you found some way to keep yourself occupied this morning," he finished up. "I would have taken you with me, even though I'm sure you would have been bored, but you were still sleeping when I left." He cocked his head at her. "You certainly do a lot of sleeping."

"Not all the time."

His expression became serious. "No. You don't."

"Brian?" she started. "Last night was everything I ever hoped it would be."

"Don't." He stopped her. "Don't you remember what the note said? One day at a time. That's how it has to be. There's just one favor I'd like to ask. I haven't been to a doctor in years. Can you recommend someone I can see when the circumstances are right?"

Because she had to honor his philosophy, Dawn

turned to a brief explanation of her morning after promising to look up the phone number of a reliable surgeon. "Everyone was at practice except for Big Bob. Coach Weatherby was going to try to run him down, but I don't know if he found out anything."

"Big Bob is asking for trouble. I have a pretty good idea of what he's up to. Look, we're due back at the field in less than an hour. I hope you don't intend on going in that outfit."

Dawn climbed out of the pool and took her towel when Brian handed it to her. Together they walked back to the motel rooms. She was hoping he'd come into her room with her, but he simply gave her a gentle kiss and took his leave.

Dawn entered her room and looked around. Housekeeping had made the bed and there were fresh towels in the bathroom. But the memory of what had happened there last night lingered in the air. No amount of cleaning could erase that.

She took her time selecting what she was going to wear. It hadn't mattered before, but now it did. She wanted it to be right for Brian. The soft, draping pale blue blouse featured a stand-up collar, pin tucks down the front, and pleated sleeves with turned-back button cuffs. She chose a slightly darker blue pair of slacks with a trim white belt and canvas sandals. The look, she thought, struck the right balance between femininity and practicality.

For once she was in a motel with a decent shower head. As a result she lingered under the spray, washing chlorine out of her hair and soaping her flesh vigorously before treating it to a long rinse. She used a generous amount of powder and a complimentary light perfume before finally opening the bathroom door to let out the steam.

That's when she saw Brian sitting on the bed. Instinctively she pulled her towel up over her breasts. She'd left her clothes on the bed, which meant she'd have to walk out into the room with only the motel towel for covering. "I didn't hear you come in," she said to cover up her embarrassment.

"I tiptoed." He glanced down at his bad knee. "At least that's one thing I can still do. Come here."

It was a command. Because she wasn't accustomed to being naked around a man, Dawn held back, but the order in Brian's eyes didn't relent. Finally, she left the relative safety of the bathroom and stepped to the bed. "It won't take me long to dress," she said nervously.

"Give me your towel." He reached up and gently pulled it from her hands. Dawn stood exposed before him, her wet hair matted against her shoulders but providing no protection from his honest gaze. A ripple of emotion flowed through her, making her unsure of what to do with her hands. Her instinct was to cover her breasts with them, but after last night the move no longer seemed right.

"Don't move. I want to look at you."

Dawn did as she was commanded. Brian's eyes traced her length slowly, completely, and yet gently. There was nothing vulgar about the way he was looking at her and that eased some of her embarrassment. "You're beautiful," he said finally.

She sought desperately for something to say, but no words formed in her mind. Instead, she reached blindly for the brief bikini panties on the bed. Brian didn't stop her but only continued to watch as, with shaking hands, she slipped into them. Next came the lacy bra.

"I didn't know," he observed.

"What?" She'd found her voice but it had little strength to it.

"What you were like under those clothes you wear. Why do you cover that femininity with baseball jerseys and jeans?"

"My job calls for jerseys and jeans." Brian's hand was resting on the remainder of her clothes. She didn't have the strength to reach for them.

"Pity. At least I know you're a woman under all that." He rose to his feet and brought her into the circle of his arms. His hands on her bare back ignited instantly the feelings she'd had last night, and she responded eagerly to his kiss. She felt exposed and vulnerable in her undergarments, and yet it added to the desire her body was surrendering to. It was impossible to pretend that Brian didn't know what his actions were doing to her senses.

I love you! Brian, I love you! The words were in danger of breaking out into the open, but with an effort Dawn held them back. One day at a time. They hadn't had enough days for the words of love to be said.

Brian's lips were on her throat, on her lightly perfumed shoulders. She was putty in his hands, completely pliable to his every whim. To remain thus in his arms for the rest of her life would have meant wanting nothing more, forever.

But just as she was wondering if the dream had a chance of fulfillment, he left off with his exploring kisses and gently ran his hands down her slender arms. "You better get dressed. We're going to be late."

For what? Dawn had to shake her head to bring herself back to the present. She dressed awkwardly, still trapped within the web of sensuality Brian had so easily wrapped her in. He watched her every move, his eyes telling nothing of his thoughts. When at last she'd slipped on her shoes, he took her hand and led her out the door.

Dawn remembered little of the drive over to the field or if they spoke on the way. She was seeing the city through a haze, streetlights, traffic, and people blurring together. The only reality was the man guiding his car through the streets.

The world imposed itself on her only once they were inside. Coach Weatherby hurried up to them, his face livid. "Big Bob isn't here. I found out that the damn fool didn't get back to the motel last night. And no one's seen him today. He was going to start. Now I've got to redo the lineup. Just wait! I'll slap a fine on him that'll make his head swim."

"Where the hell is he?" Brian's words were as harsh as earlier they'd been tender. "Doesn't he know he's already walking a fine line with us?"

"I don't think he cares." The manager shook his head angrily. "The idiot thinks he's above reproach. Just because he got into college on a sports scholarship and now has a contract, he thinks he can do no wrong."

"I'm sure he was on drugs during the first game," Dawn offered. "Either that or he'd been drinking. Do you think it's that again?"

"It wouldn't surprise me," Brian said before taking off.

Dawn didn't see Brian again until the end of the game. Early on a base runner jammed his ankle sliding into base, and Dawn missed the rest of the game because she had to administer ice packs to the uncomfortable player. He kept insisting that he was ready to get back in the game. It was only by staying with him that Dawn could be sure he wouldn't try to walk on his rapidly swelling ankle. She was irritated with the athlete's disregard for what could become a serious injury if not treated, and yet she understood. Of course he wanted to play. That's why he was here, wasn't it?

She didn't realize how long she'd been in the locker room until she heard the rest of the team trooping in. From the looks on their faces she knew they'd won. They were also, to a man, thoroughly fed up with Big Bob.

"He came sauntering into the dugout halfway through the sixth inning," Coach Weatherby explained. "Dressed for action and complaining because someone else was on his base. I told him he was more than a little late, but he didn't care. He kept saying he'd been slotted to start and now that he was here I had to put him in."

"What did you do?" Dawn asked.

"I told him to take a walk. That's after I slapped him with a fine that made his mouth drop open. I don't play games with irresponsible people. If he can't be where he's supposed to be, when he's supposed to, I'm not about to pat him on the back. What really sealed my decision was that he told me it was none of my damn business where he'd been all that time. Hell! I'm not being paid to listen to that garbage.''

"Did you fire him?" Dawn was relieved that she hadn't been there. She probably would have jumped on Bob herself. It was obvious the manager could handle matters without her help.

"Not yet. But it's probably coming. We don't need a crazy man, no matter how good his mitt is. In this man's game you either play by the rules or you don't play at all."

"What's going to happen?" Dawn pressed. "Is he going to be given a second chance? Is he on suspension? I know it's your decision. I just think he's already had enough warning."

"I told him he's meeting with Brian and me as soon as we get back to the Rogue Valley."

A minute later Dawn left the locker room to give the players a chance to change. She was depressed by what had happened with Big Bob. For the most part she was quite fond of the young athletes, despite their high jinks. It pained her to think that one of them was in danger of throwing away his career. She couldn't dismiss her suspicion that drugs were at the root of Bob's behavior. She'd seen him high just once, but some things the other players said from time to time had her convinced that it wasn't an isolated incident.

And after my lecture too, she fumed even as she admitted that lectures weren't the best way of making a point. Dawn believed that using drugs was the same as playing with fire. Why couldn't Big Bob see that?

Irritation over the rebellious ballplayer didn't last long. That feeling was soon replaced by a depression she hid from the others but not from her heart. She had to return to the motel with the team because there was no sign of Brian after the game. She tried to find an explanation for his disappearance until she learned from the motel clerk that the team's general manager had already checked out of the motel. Although the team had three more games to play on their road trip, it was clear that Brian had more important matters on his mind than staying with them— with her. True, the clerk had made mention of a long-distance message, followed by his hasty departure, but Dawn couldn't understand why he'd leave without getting in touch with her.

Dawn spent too much of the night tossing and turning, hurting because he hadn't offered her an explanation. He should have taken her with him. It would have meant sitting together during a trip that took most of the night, but was being in the same car with her so hard to take? After what had passed between them on this trip, she prayed that the barriers had started to fall and they'd reach that measure of closeness lovers are privy to.

But Brian didn't want to be around her. In her heart there was no other explanation for his behavior.

She should have known, she thought as she gratefully watched the morning sun bring an end to the long night. One night in Brian's arms was no guarantee that he felt as she did. He'd had second thoughts, and this was his way of letting her know that the magic night they'd shared was a mistake.

It hurt. More than she could ever let him know.

Dawn was silent and withdrawn during the long trip back to Verdue Field four days later. Coach Weatherby tried to engage her in conversation but eventually left her alone to deal with her wounded heart. The hectic pace of the past few days had done nothing to ease the pain; she hadn't expected it to. She was dimly aware that Big Bob was sitting apart from the other players and wondered if they were avoiding him. His face wore a hard, defensive look, but in her present state Dawn felt ill-equipped to deal with a man who had so little regard for his career. How could she tell him to take control of his life when she felt as if she were drowning in her own?

What was it Brian wanted? Did he expect their professional relationship to continue while pretending that the hours in each other's arms never happened? Was he going to ask that of her? Or would he avoid her completely? And, was it possible that she was reading too much into his sudden disappearance? Maybe something pressing had indeed come up and he'd had to deal with that. Maybe she'd get back to Verdue Field only to find him ignorant of the turmoil he'd put her through.

Could she really believe that?

Brian wasn't at Verdue Field when the team bus finally pulled up and the weary men stretched and climbed off. Dawn was the last to leave, torn between the need to see Brian and fear of what she might find when at last they were face to face. If he told her—as she now feared—that their lovemaking was a mistake, would she have the courage to accept what she couldn't change? What made her think she was entitled to that grand slam feeling? No, this was closer to a strikeout with the bases loaded.

In a way she was relieved to find the parking lot

empty of the Verdue Field van. It delayed the inevitable. She used her field key to unlock Brian's office and looked up the phone number of a surgeon she felt had the expertise with Brian's problem. She used a notepad on his desk and copied down Dr. Halston's name and number and left it with a brief note near the phone. Finally, she climbed into her car, rolled down the window to let out the trapped heat, and drove home to a cooling shower.

Although she prepared a fruit salad, it failed to revive her appetite. In desperation she went jogging, and then turned in early that evening. The phone remained a taunting challenge, daring her to call Brian's number. She turned her back on that challenge.

With another game set for that evening, Dawn woke to a day already outlined for her. The players would be affected by the inactivity brought on by the time spent on a bus and in need of exercises especially designed to bring their muscles back to peak efficiency. Dawn was determined to let the manager and Brian know that she hadn't changed her mind about Big Bob. She wasn't in a position to fire anyone, but her personal conviction was that Bob either seek professional help or be removed from the team. That might be harsh, but the player was of little use to the team as he was now and in fact was capable of damaging the entire team's morale. She wondered if Brian might already be aware of how serious Bob's problem was and had already acted.

The answer was made obvious when Dawn had been on the playing field for less than five minutes. Like a forest fire whipped by wind, the news of Bob's suspension spread through the team as they went through their limbering-up exercises. "I saw him in the office with Brian when I got here this morning," one of the pitchers was telling everyone within earshot. "He wasn't in there long when he came storming out yelling at Brian that he couldn't get away with something. Big Bob said something about Brian being sorry, that he wasn't going to lie down like a whipped dog and take it on the chin."

"What about Brian?" Dawn asked. "How did he react?"

"A hell of a lot calmer than I would have," the lanky blonde explained. "Brian suggested Bob get in touch with his agent, but until Bob could prove he was done with drugs, there wasn't any place for him on the team. I have to give Brian credit. I would have fired that jerk on the spot, but Brian left the door opened. Said something about Bob needing medical care and that Brian would stand behind him if he sincerely wanted help. I don't think Bob was listening, though. He was too busy making threats."

Dawn could almost hear Brian speaking. She knew how his voice sounded when he was deeply concerned. Hadn't she seen his eyes deepen and his voice become low pitched when he talked about his determination to gain custody of Tad?

Dawn faced the evening with a dread she couldn't ignore. She expected Brian to be on hand for the game, which meant he'd have to acknowledge her presence. But what form would that acknowledgement take? Would he be coolly detached? Would he leave it up to her to figure out why their relationship had begun with such blazing promise only to die like a plant left unwatered? Or would his honesty be so brutal that she was left devastated?

And yet she still carried inside her a dream that was as hopeless as it was persistent. She closed her eyes and imagined Brian taking her in his arms, full of easily accepted explanations for his sudden departure and the silence that grew even more disturbing as time passed.

Dawn dressed in a green blouse and white slacks to reflect the team's colors. She considered tying her hair back, but its length brushing her cheeks and neck was comforting and she left it to drape loosely. She wrinkled her nose because she knew she was risking ruin to her slacks in the well-used dugout, reached for her keys, and closed the door on the rooms that were too confining for her thoughts.

The noises that were part of a ball field gearing up for nine innings of action helped to revive her. Her spirit was further lifted by the high-spirited attitude of the players. They were young, full of life's promise. They didn't dwell long on the misfortunes of others.

Brian was there. From her station in the dugout Dawn caught only glimpses of him as he went about his business, but there was no doubting the reason for the animated look on his face. Tad was with him. The boy obviously loved being the center of attention, not only with his father, but also with the many people Brian stopped to talk to as he made his way through the stands. Dawn's heart did a flip at the sight of Brian dressed in a white knit pullover shirt with green running down the shirt's sleeves. Dawn hadn't seen the shirt before and surmised that he'd bought it so fans could identify him as someone associated with the team. She wondered if he noticed that she too was wearing the team's colors, but because he came nowhere near the dugout, she had no opportunity to ask him.

The game was one of those rare pitchers' duels that appeal to the true baseball statistician but was often boring to the spectator interested in action. Dawn watched the pitcher closely for signs of tiring, but the powerfully built young man was working like a well-oiled machine, his curves breaking perfectly and his fast balls slapping resoundingly into the catcher's mitt.

"This kid's going to be moving up," Coach Weatherby whispered to her. Dawn nodded, happy for the dedicated young man on the mound. She'd watched him throwing at a mitt-sized target for hours on end, perfecting his control. It was this kind of dedication that Dawn loved to see. For a moment she thought of Jim and the hours and days and weeks he'd spent bringing himself back from being confined to a bed and wondered if his life was reflecting the rewards of that work. She hoped so. She just wasn't sure she could say the same for herself.

Oh, she had a challenging, fulfilling job that allowed her to remain out of doors in the company of high-spirited young men. She was no longer hemmed in by skyscrapers. But a job and pleasant surroundings didn't make a whole life.

When the game finally ended, she slowly gathered the tools of her trade and made her way out of the dugout. She had started toward the training room when a whirlpool of activity dove at her, almost knocking her off balance as Tad wrapped his arms around her legs.

"I've been looking for you," he said. "Where have you been?"

"Where do you think?" She dropped her load and lifted the boy onto her hip, oblivious to his tennis shoes leaving dirt tracks on her white slacks. "I was hiding in here so I didn't have to buy you any more ice-cream cones. How are you, Tad? What are you doing here?"

"I'm here with my daddy." The words were spoken with such love that for a moment she couldn't trust herself to speak. Instead, she lifted her eyes and came face to face with Brian.

After a thousand imagined conversations, Dawn had nothing to say. Brian broke the silence. "That was a good game. Tad got a little bored, but then he likes home runs. He even applauds errors."

Dawn could only stare. No word, nothing from Brian for too long, and now he was speaking as if they were no more than casual friends. He'd had her on the brink of tears a half dozen times since the last time they were together, but at the moment tears were the last thing on her mind. "I'm glad Tad's here," she said casually.

"It wasn't easy." Brian lowered his voice so it wouldn't carry. "I've been with my lawyer every free minute, working out the details so I can have Tad on a temporary basis until the custody hearing. Something came up." He dipped his head at his son, telling her that now wasn't the time to explain further. "Tad needs security in his life."

"Oh." She wanted to wish him good luck, to tell him she believed that being with his father was the best thing for the boy wrapped around her neck. She also wanted to ask why she'd been left out of this aspect of his life. But she held back. This was a deeply personal matter, not something to be discussed with other people around. "Did you get my note about a surgeon? Are you going to make an appointment?"

"I already did." Brian pulled her out of the stream of people heading for the exit. His hand on her shoulder was an instant electrical charge, but she held herself firmly against responding to it. "I'm going to see him next week, but it doesn't matter what he says. No surgery until I know whether I'm going to get Tad. I'm not going to risk giving my ex's attorney anything he can use against me."

She nodded. "Just don't put it off any longer than you have to. It isn't going to get better."

"Yes, Nurse." Brian held out his arms to receive Tad. "Look, I've got to get this dynamo home. It's long past his bedtime."

Dawn stared after his already retreating figure. "Brian."

He stopped. "What?"

"Don't you think I deserve some kind of explanation?" Her question was forced out on the forefront of her confused emotions. "I don't understand what's happening."

"I'll get in touch with you tomorrow, when there aren't little ears around. We have a lot to talk about. There are some things you need to understand."

"I agree. We have to talk." She took a deep breath. "What I don't understand is why you didn't get in touch with me."

"Tomorrow," Brian repeated. "Things have been very hectic for me."

Dawn stood staring after Brian's retreating back. She could understand that Brian had a lot on his mind. But what she couldn't understand was why he hadn't found a few minutes for her.

Stop it! she told herself. Dawn shook her head. She could be reading too much into their lovemaking. He hadn't placed a ring on her finger; neither had she asked for a lifetime commitment before going to bed with him. Brian didn't owe her anything.

Chapter Ten

Dawn slept better than she had for two nights. Whether it was because her body's needs finally ruled over her thoughts or because she'd made a certain peace with herself she wasn't sure. All she knew was that it felt good to wake up determined to take the day as it came instead of agonizing over what might or might not happen. Brian said they needed to talk. But until they were face to face, she wasn't going to let it ruin what was a perfect spring morning.

She extended her jogging by another mile, treated herself to a cool shower followed by a liberal application of rose-scented perfume, and finally gave herself the rare treat of breakfast at a sunlit restaurant where strawberry crepes were the specialty. She was feeling uncomfortably full and slightly sinful when she arrived at Verdue Field. Practice went well, and except for having to attend to a happy pitcher with a decidedly sore arm, her chores were minimal. She tried to chide the young man for going the distance instead of giving way to a relief pitcher, but even as she pasted a stern expression on her face she had to admit she probably would have reacted in the same way if she'd been in his place. "Just looking for all the glory you can get, aren't you?" she asked as his arm was being treated to a whirlpool bath. "You're probably thinking your mug's going to be on the front page of the paper, aren't you?"

"All I want is the top half of the sports section." The pitcher forced his face into an idiotic ear-to-ear grin. "I want to send it back to my folks and a certain girl."

"It'll probably be a picture of you trying to stab at the line drive that just about knocked you off the mound. You're just lucky the shortstop was there to back you up."

The pitcher gave her a look that said that particular incident was something he didn't want to talk about and then launched into a description of his career, which began in Little League at age eight. "I've always known what I've wanted."

I've known what I've wanted for ten years, Dawn's heart said before she could clamp a lid on it. To keep her feelings from getting the upper hand again she pressed the pitcher for more information about his high school years, keeping him talking until they were joined by several players who had suddenly developed sore elbows in a blatant attempt to get to use the whirlpool bath.

When the team broke for lunch, Dawn drove to the shopping center and forced herself to stick to business until she'd found a pair of shoes that didn't require white laces. The clerk, an overbearing man in his thirties, made several comments about her well-muscled legs, but Dawn recognized the ill-concealed proposition and let his words hang unanswered.

She was on her way back to her car when she spotted a newspaper boy loading a coin-operated dispenser with the day's paper and bought a copy to read when she got home.

She fixed herself a tall glass of iced tea and was propping her bare feet up on the coffee table when she opened the paper to the sports section. There was a picture of the young pitcher she'd been talking to earlier, but his exploits were given smaller billing than the other article on the page.

NORTHWEST LEAGUE GENERAL MANAGER FACES CRIPPLING INJURY. Beneath that blazing headline ran a smaller one that suggested Brian was trying to hide his condition. The body of the article, written by Ralph, named an "inside" source who reluctantly admitted that Brian had been experiencing extreme pain in a knee that had already been under the knife but was putting off treatment. The reason for the delay wasn't spelled out, but the hint was that it was because he didn't want to put himself in hospital so soon after the start of the season. The last paragraph turned Dawn's blood cold.

The informed source expressed fear that it might already be too late for surgery to rectify the problem. It would indeed be a tragedy if such a vital man was forced to spend the rest of his life as a cripple.

Who was this source? she wondered. Except for herself, Dawn couldn't think of anyone else who knew about Brian's knee. She supposed it was possible that Brian had confided in Coach Weatherby, but she couldn't imagine the craggy older man letting that slip around Ralph.

Dawn almost picked up the phone to call Ralph but decided against it. The damage was done. What good would it do for her to tell the man that the article had nothing to do with his responsibilities as a sports reporter and was in extremely bad taste? She'd always associated terms like *unidentified source* with the kind of articles that were coming out about public figures, articles usually so twisted that only the totally gullible would believe them. Brian had made an appointment, but the doctor hadn't actually seen him yet so Dawn couldn't imagine that the article had anything to do with the surgeon Dawn had referred Brian to.

Dawn threw the paper across the room and stared at it, shaking. She'd never had a very high opinion of Ralph, but this was unforgivable!

The sound of the settling pages was echoed by an insistent knock at her front door. Dawn jumped. Her nerves were already on edge because of what she'd just read. She hoped it wouldn't be a salesman. She wasn't in the mood for a polite refusal of what he was selling.

Instead of a stranger, Dawn opened the door to a hard-faced Brian. In his hand he carried the sports section. He waved it in her face, forcing her away from the door as he stepped in. "What the hell did you do that for? God, don't you have any idea what you've done?"

"You think I—" The thought stopped her words in her throat.

"You're damn right!" Brian raged. He kicked at the door with his foot, slamming it behind him. "Who else could it be? Do you really think you could hide behind the 'unidentified source' garbage?''

The anger in Brian's eyes ignited a like emotion in Dawn, but she kept a firm grip on her temper and concentrated on logic, or rather the lack of logic. "Why did Ralph have to say that about you being a cripple? That's crazy."

"You're the one who put that crazy idea in his head! Don't blame Ralph for an overactive imagination. He hasn't had an original idea for years."

"Wait a minute." Dawn held up a hand to ward off the sparks flashing from Brian's eyes and forced herself to remain calm. "You have it all wrong. You can't believe I—"

"Knock it off!" Brian pushed against her chest until she was forced to collapse, unceremoniously, onto her couch. "You might as well save your breath, Dawn. I'm not interested in any explanation, any apology. It's too late for that. Dammit! Why?"

"Why?" Her mouth sagged. Was she really hearing those words? "I can't believe—"

"You can't believe I wouldn't take this sitting down? What is it, Dawn? Do you hate me? Okay." He ran a large white-knuckled hand through his hair. "Maybe I should have gotten in touch with you the other day, told you why I was so short of time. I'm sorry I didn't call or leave a note. But you didn't have to do that to me." He threw the paper at her.

"Why were you short of time?" Maybe she was going about this all wrong, but she felt she had to counter his anger with calmness and logic, or at least as much as she was capable of.

"What does it matter now? All right. You want to

know? Maybe you'll understand. Tad ran away from home while we were on that road trip. His mother called and left a message for me at the motel. I took off the minute I got it.''

"Why didn't you tell me?''

Again he pulled at his hair. "Tad was back home when I got there. He'd spent the night hiding in his friend's backyard. But that was the trigger. It was time for action. I told my lawyer I wasn't going to let the custody question drag out any longer. I want Tad. That's where I've been for the past few days. Trying to get the legal wheels rolling. But you've probably destroyed that.''

Dawn grabbed the paper tightly, wrinkling it because she felt as if she were going to explode. "What does this article have to do with Tad?''

"You don't see it? Even now you don't see it?'' He looked a breath away from striking her. "God, don't you know what Tad's mother's lawyer is going to do with this? He's going to try to convince the judge that I'm a cripple. And a cripple can't raise a child. Her lies are bad enough. But now I have to fight this.''

"And you think I'm responsible? You really think that of me?''

"What else can I think?'' He was looming over her like some avenger out of a horror movie. "No one else knows about my knee. Just you.'' He shook his head like an animal who had received a blow to the head. "I came here because I had to know why you felt it necessary to say anything to Ralph. I was going to drag it out of you if need be. Now—now I don't care anymore.''

Dawn stared unwaveringly at Brian, feeling everything—and nothing. If Brian believed she was capable of deceiving him, there simply wasn't anything left to fight for. "I don't either, Brian," she said through the tight lines of her lips. "Go ahead. Hate me. I'm not going to try to stop you. In your eyes I'm guilty. That's what it boils down to, isn't it?"

A puzzled expression appeared momentarily in Brian's eyes, but it was quickly replaced by the look of a man who'd exposed, too much of himself and was drawing back. Without speaking he turned and left.

For a long time Dawn simply stared at the door that had taken Brian away from her. If she had any emotions, she was unaware of them. Some great numbness had stretched itself over and around her until she was incapable of moving, or feeling. Her head fell backward and rested against the back of the couch.

She closed her eyes in an instinctive attempt to block out the sight of his raging features. But instead of feeling the insulation she craved, his eyes came to haunt her even more than they had before.

Brian hated her.

No matter what else she might think that day, only one fact had any reality. Brian hated her. It didn't matter that he was totally wrong in the conclusion he'd jumped to and that she might, if she tried hard enough, be able to convince him of her innocence. What did it matter? If he could believe her capable of such a vile act, she simply no longer cared enough to try to fight his belief.

But what made it impossible for her to rise from the couch was the one simple fact that continued to pound through her with every heartbeat. She still loved him.

It made no sense. How could she continue to have feelings for a man who'd assaulted her senses, her emotions, so cruelly? By all rights she should be cursing his name and throwing things at the closed door.

But she didn't. Deep in that sheltered part of her heart where lived the core of her love, the ember still flickered. He was a man capable of the full range of human emotions. His anger was only one facet of those emotions, not enough to destroy the feelings that had taken seed because he was much, much more than raging eyes and accusations.

When it seemed as if the day were going to end without her moving again, Dawn summoned the strength to push herself to her feet. She pressed a hand to her hot, aching head and stumbled into the bedroom. She fell facedownward onto her bed, but the tears she expected to fall only continued to build up inside until she wondered if she was going to shatter from the pressure.

Brian hated her. Again she'd been ejected from his ball park.

And she continued to love him.

She might have spent the rest of the early evening facedown on her bed if it hadn't been for the 7:30 P.M. game time. Slowly, painfully, she sat up and stumbled into the bathroom. Her face in the mirror shocked her. It was white with dark hollows for eyes. It didn't seem possible that she could have lost her tan in a matter of an hour, but gone was the bronzed look that gave her face the needed contrast to her ivory hair.

Brian once called her an angel in white. Tonight she more closely resembled a ghost—the ghost of a living woman.

Dawn stripped slowly, dropping her clothes in an unattended heap on the bathroom floor, and stepped into the shower. As the tepid water beat against her sensitive flesh she finally found release for the tears she'd been denied before. She shampooed her hair, sobbing under cover of the torrent of falling water. She stood motionless under the spray for another five minutes, arms hanging limply at her sides, wilted, until her tears had spent themselves.

Dawn felt rung out, emotionally exhausted when finally she stepped out and grabbed the terry cloth towel she'd bought because it was large enough to totally envelop her. She used another towel to wrap her hair in and then stepped out of the bathroom and back into her bedroom. The carpet under her bare feet felt warm and soft, insulation for her flesh if not for her heart.

The sight that greeted her in the mirror was even more disheartening than before. Now, in addition to a telltale pallor to her skin, her red eyes gave away the agony she felt in her heart. There was no turning away from the reality in the mirror.

"You fool! No matter what he believes, you still love him!"

She chose a white silk blouse because anything else would feel harsh on her flesh. She zipped herself into a slim pair of slacks and shoved her feet into the shoes she'd bought earlier in the day—before her world had fallen down around her. Makeup was almost more than she could concentrate on, but because she wanted to hide the heartache that showed in her eyes, she took the time to conceal her emotions with eye shadow and mascara. Because she'd never been in the habit of wearing powder or blusher, she had nothing with which to coax life back into her cheeks. Finally, she blow-dried her hair until most of the moisture was out of it, and surveyed the result.

The Dawn who'd spent a night in Brian's arms no longer existed. She didn't recognize the pale ghost in its place.

She remembered nothing of the short drive to Verdue Field and little more of the next four hours. She tried to lose herself in the team's upbeat mood as it became clear that they were going to win the game going away, but a small measure of her remained locked away. That part could think only of raging eyes and accusing words.

If Brian was at Verdue Field that night, she didn't see him. She kept her eyes resolutely on the field, concentrating as best she could on the conversations swirling around her. The dugout and the life resounding through it were her salvation. Surrounded by vibrant young men she could manage her heartache, put it on hold until she was once again alone.

Coach Weatherby insisted on hovering over her. "My wife looked like that when our son was in a bicycle accident. I thought I was going to have to admit her to the hospital too. I don't suppose you want to talk about it."

Dawn shook her head. "Thank you. But it's personal."

"I kind of figured that." He patted her on the shoulder. "Did you see the article Ralph wrote? I wouldn't put it past him to have made up the whole thing. I've heard via the grapevine that he's barely holding on to his job. This must be his way of trying to look good with his editor. It's the big exposé that sells papers. I just hope to hell Brian sues him."

"You don't believe what Ralph said about an un-identified source?" Dawn asked.

"Who knows?" The manager shrugged. "I know Brian's knee is giving him trouble. I've even heard some of the kids say they thought he had a limp. But Brian's not anywhere near a wheelchair. That's a pack of lies."

Dawn met the manager's eyes. "We know that. But Brian could have a hard time convincing a judge of that."

"You're talking about custody of Tad." Coach Weatherby winked. "You look surprised. Brian doesn't talk much about his personal life, but I know how he is around that boy of his. He wants Tad living with him. He'd be good for the boy. That article is going to make it harder. There's no question of that."

"Why did Ralph do it?" Dawn pressed.

"Who knows why Ralph does anything? Look, if I know Brian, he's just starting to fight. He's not going to let that damn article make him holler uncle. Don't you worry about it, young lady." The manager again patted her shoulder. "We're talking about a man with the guts to fight for what he wants."

But Coach Weatherby's words didn't give Dawn the peace she needed. She kept thinking about what Ralph had written. The article had said that Brian was facing a future tied to a wheelchair. There was something about written words that gave them the ring of authority. Would Brian be able to convince a judge that there was no truth to the story?

Dawn had to deal with a jammed thumb and a foreign body in the shortstop's eye, which kept her at Verdue Field an hour after the game had ended. She had no reason to hurry; there was no one waiting to see her, no one who wanted to take her in his arms. When she finally locked the treatment room door behind her, she turned to face a silent, deserted Verdue Field. Instead of going to her car, she walked out onto the field, her thoughts tumbling in confusion around her. Night was supposed to bring peace, wasn't it? The cold air on her face should be washing away the lethargy she was trapped in. But it wasn't turning out that way. The night air offered no escape from the walls her thoughts kept crashing into.

One day at a time, Brian had offered her. But their one day—their one night—was over.

What was left was a little house and nothing to break the silence she brought to it.

Dawn slept little, if at all. She was helpless to free herself from the image of a man bending to hear the laughter of the boy at his side. The look on the man's face was mirrored by the child—a look of love. No wonder Brian had attacked her. He believed her the one who was threatening that precious relationship.

And she'd done nothing to deny it.

It was barely light when the phone rang. Dawn fought her way out of her half-slumbering state and grabbed the receiver, hoping despite all odds that she'd hear Brian's voice.

Instead, it was her mother. "What are you doing today?" Crystal asked, her words coming together in a rush. "I know there's no game tonight. Is there any chance you have some free time?"

The rest of my life, Dawn thought. "Probably," she

said, careful to keep her tone light. "Did you have anything in mind."

"How would you like to attend a wedding?"

"Mom!" Dawn sat upright and swung her legs out of bed. "Are you serious?"

"Do you think I'd joke about a thing like this? Peter and I want to get married. Today. And I'd like to have my daughter stand up with me."

"Oh—" Dawn cringed at how the word sounded, but she had little control over her reaction to the events swirling around her.

"Dawn? You don't mind, do you? I mean, your father—"

"Dad would have wanted you happy," Dawn reassured her mother. "I'm sorry. It's just that my life's pretty mixed up these days. I'm just a little slow in reacting, that's all. You're right. There isn't a game today. There's nothing I'd like more than to see my mother get married."

After a short conversation, the two women hung up. Dawn flopped back on her bed. Her mother was getting married! As the realization sank in, tears stung her eyes. Tears of happiness for her mother. Tears because it was the mother and not the daughter who was linking her heart and life with another.

But today was for Crystal Morrell. Dawn opened her eyes and stared at the ceiling as she collected her thoughts. She had to put Brian and their last confrontation behind her today. Her mother deserved all possible happiness. And Dawn was determined to be part of the day that would launch that happiness.

An hour later she was pulling up at her mother's house. The ceremony was to be a simple one, held at a small wedding chapel out in the country. Dawn remembered driving by the chapel when she was a child and dreaming of the day when she might be the bride standing under the vine-covered arch in the side yard. Dawn had often wondered who was responsible for the healthy greenery tied to a redwood frame that served as the backdrop for outdoor weddings. A church wedding had its own special meaning, but because Dawn so loved the out-of-doors, she'd always carried the hope that she'd have a reason to stand here one day.

The only part of her dream that wasn't going to come true today was that she wasn't the bride.

"I can't believe how nervous I am," her mother groaned as Dawn was helping with her hair. "Peter and I agreed that at our age an elaborate affair wouldn't be right. There's just going to be you and Peter's brother with us." Crystal stared at her trembling hands. "I'm acting like I'm going to be on national television."

"Take a deep breath," Dawn ordered, pushing her mother into a chair because it was the only way to get her to keep still. "You're making me nervous too."

"I'm sorry. I can't help it."

"That's all right. And it's natural to be nervous. After all, that's a pretty big step you two are taking."

"Don't remind me." Crystal groaned again. "I just wish I felt the way I did when we decided we were too much in love not to get married. I wonder if every bride feels this way on her wedding day, no matter how many she's had."

"Probably." Dawn fell silent. Her thoughts went back in time, past the recent weeks, through the

years, until she was once again a teenager. Had there
ever been a time when she didn't know her heart belonged to Brian? she questioned. Maybe the feeling
had found its way into the quiet back roads of her
mind during the years when they were apart, but she
rather believed the feeling had always been there.
Like a caterpillar sleeping its way through the cocoon
stage, her love had simmered under the surface. But it
was there.

It still was.

"Love's a mysterious thing," Dawn said softly.
"We can't hold it in our hands. We can't put it under
a microscope and examine it. But the word, the feeling, has meaning for everyone."

"You're being awfully profound today. I didn't
know my getting married would have such an impact
on you," Crystal said.

"It's all your fault," Dawn quipped. "If you hadn't
read *Cinderella* to me so many times, I wouldn't be
such an incurable romantic. Prince Charming? I really
believed there was a man with that name." She blinked
back sudden tears and forced a smile. "You look beautiful. Now, let's make you into a married woman."

Crystal Morrell did indeed make a beautiful bride.
As Dawn watched her mother link her hand with
Peter and repeat the vows that made them man and
wife, she gave up the struggle.

It could be her and Brian there. The fantasy she was
spinning in the little chapel's garden could have become reality for Dawn and Brian if it hadn't been for
yesterday. They could be the ones sealing their love
with a kiss and a vow, placing rings on each other's
fingers, gazing into each other's eyes.

Dawn trembled, beyond tears, as her heart whispered the vows her mother was saying. She dropped her head as Crystal lifted her lips to her new husband. She was happy for her mother because she had been given the precious gift of two loves in her life. In her heart Dawn knew that no disservice had been done to her father's memory. Her parents had loved each other with a love that endured through one lifetime. Her father was dead, but her mother was still alive in all the ways that counted. It would be sad if Crystal had no one to share that precious life with.

Dawn waited until the marriage kiss was over and then embraced her mother. "I'm so happy for you," she whispered around her tears. "I hope you know that."

Crystal held her daughter's hands. "This is what I want for you too," she whispered back. "Love is the greatest gift anyone can receive."

When at last the celebration dinner was over and Crystal and Peter were launched on their honeymoon, Dawn tried to shake off her mother's words. She had fought to maintain her composure during the candlelit dinner when the newlyweds could barely keep their eyes off each other, but now composure no longer mattered.

Dawn was back in the little house that brought her so much satisfaction when she first moved into it. It seemed doubly lonely now. It wasn't just because she'd been to a wedding. The memory of Brian's last words to her continued to haunt her. He'd come to demand the truth from her. But he'd left with an inescapable message. *"I don't care anymore."*

And she still did.

Dawn slept fitfully and rose early. She dressed automatically, yanking on the elastic waist of her jogging outfit and roughly pulling a terry top over her tangled hair. She hadn't had the chance to go running yesterday and her muscles cried out for exercise.

It was still more night than day when she locked the door behind her and started down the quiet street. As her running shoes pounded on the pavement she emptied her mind of the thoughts that made the night endless. She lifted her face to receive the cool rush of air, feeling the color being brought back into her cheeks.

In retrospect yesterday had served as the break she so desperately needed from her thoughts and emotions. Despite her quiet sorrow because her father wasn't part of their life anymore, Dawn realized that the wedding had helped to lift her out of the hopeless mire of her thoughts. She didn't yet know where her new thoughts and feelings were taking her, but no longer did she feel a helpless prisoner in the face of Brian's anger.

Her fight was coming back.

With more purpose than accident Dawn's route took her to Verdue Field. She trotted across the gravel parking lot and came to the small side door used by the maintenance crew. It opened at her touch and she stepped inside the stadium that had filled her with so much hope for the future a few short weeks ago.

Once she was past the maze of bleachers she saw that the grounds crew had set the sprinklers, which were now catching the morning sun in their sparkling mist. Dawn stood motionless, watching the play of light on water, feeling the promise of heat the day held. Verdue Field. No other name would have fulfilled the land's promise. It was a green paradise. From where she stood she could feel the fine spray touch her face. She lifted her head and closed her eyes, remembering. A man with a small child's hand securely in his. A man with the ability to turn her body into fire.

Dawn opened her eyes and stared again at the high, moving arc of water as it dampened the endless green carpet. She remembered a motorcycle ride that had ended in a shower of gravel and pain and screaming sirens. That was followed by weeks of immobility, weeks of not knowing what future, if any, Jim had to look forward to. She had no desire to deny the slow, strong, steady change in her life. She'd faced up to the fact that she could never find her own personal peace within a hospital setting. Fulfillment for her meant helping bodies retain whatever degree of health they were capable of.

It hadn't been easy. It still hurt to remember the months of work it took to put Jim back on his feet.

But Jim was working now. The accident had taught him something about himself as well. The carefree youth who lived for momentary pleasures had matured into a man who was ready to become a responsible member of society. When Dawn and Jim parted, it was without pain because reality had matured them.

Could she expect any less of herself now?

Maybe the dreams she had of Brian would never be more than dreams. Maybe too much damage had been wrought for them to be able to weave their lives together as Crystal and Peter had done.

But Brian had a need for, a right to his son. Just as

Jim had a need, a right to walk. Dawn had been able to offer a helping hand to Jim. Could she do any less for the man she would always love?

Dawn walked onto Verdue Field, the dampness soaking through her cloth shoes. Cold spray struck her exposed flesh, but she didn't flinch from it. She needed—craved even—the cleansing power of the water. In Chicago she'd watched one man fight for what he needed to remain alive. Brian had that same fight in him. And it was Tad he needed to feel alive, not her. Maybe not her ever. But there was no doubting the power of his feelings for his son.

One newspaper article couldn't spell the end to a father-son relationship. Maybe Dawn hadn't had any part in that article, but then she hadn't done anything to cut through the lies that implicated her.

It was time for her to put an end to inaction. Somehow, she wasn't sure how yet, she'd reveal the lies for what they were. She'd do what she could for Tad and his father.

And after that? she wondered.

Dawn lifted her face so the fine spray glistened off her ivory hair. There would be time enough then to decide whether there was anything left of what they had started.

Chapter Eleven

Dawn's courage almost failed her as she drove through the city and found an empty parking lot within a block of the *Nugget* office. When she'd called earlier to ask if Ralph was in, the receptionist wanted to make an appointment, but Dawn had the suspicion she was the last person Ralph wanted to see. At least she learned that Ralph was due to spend the morning in his office, writing his articles for the day's paper.

She locked her car, pulled down on the lightweight top that had stuck to her during the warm ride over, and squared her shoulders. It was rather like facing the lion in his den, she admitted, wondering if the apprehension she felt in the pit of her stomach showed in her eyes.

Why should she be nervous? she thought as the receptionist pointed her in the direction of the sports department. It was Ralph who was playing with Brian's future. Dawn found it hard to conceive that Ralph wasn't aware of the possible ramifications of his irresponsible article. The state of Brian's knee had nothing to do with sports and the Northwest League.

It was an underhanded attempt to sell newspapers and nothing more.

Ralph had a small cubicle set apart from the main newsroom. A glass enclosure gave him a measure of privacy, and yet he and whoever he might have in with him could watch everything that was happening in the crowded, noisy room. Dawn stopped for a moment. She'd never been inside a city newsroom before. She hadn't known what to expect, but she wasn't prepared for what seemed to be total disorganization made even more so by desks overflowing with stacks of paper. If she hadn't been determined to get her visit with Ralph over with as soon as possible, she would have been tempted to peek over shoulders to try to determine how anyone could concentrate under these conditions.

Ralph looked intent on what he was reading and didn't look up until Dawn rapped on the glass door. If he was surprised to see her, he hid it well.

"I guess I shouldn't be surprised. This is my lucky day. I'm getting all kinds of visitors. You're a little early, young lady." He led her inside and closed the door. "Not that I'm complaining, of course. You, I'm always glad to see."

"You might not be when I'm done," she said shortly, forcing all emotion into the background. Now was the time for logic, not anger, she knew. "Do you have any idea why I'm here?" Why he thought she was early was beyond her, but she didn't want to get sidetracked thinking about that.

"Let me guess. Does it have something to do with a certain gentleman of your acquaintance?" Ralph's eyes slid lazily down her body, making her uncomfortably aware of the static electricity that bonded her nylon top to her breasts.

"Why did you do it?" No! She hadn't meant to say anything that would put him on the defensive.

"Why did I write the article?" Ralph shrugged and sank back in his chair. "It seemed like the thing to do."

Since it was obvious that Ralph wasn't enough of a gentleman to offer her a seat, Dawn located a plastic-molded one against a wall and pulled it close to his desk before sitting down. She wasn't about to stand around awkwardly while Ralph relaxed. "I want to know where you got your information, or rather what little fact there was in that—that piece of nonsense."

"Nonsense?" Ralph's lips curled in warning. "I don't take kindly to having my writing criticized in that manner."

"What would you prefer I call it?" she asked, her eyes meeting his challenge. She wasn't afraid of Ralph, just disgusted. The sparring contest they were engaged in might not quickly give her the information she needed, but if she could find a crack in his cynical armor, she was determined to make the most of it. "I believe the term *yellow journalism* has a place here."

The frown on Ralph's face darkened. "I don't know why you've decided to jump to Riegel's defense. Perhaps that's what we should be discussing, not my literary talents."

"You call that literary? It's nothing but a pack of lies!"

"And how would you know that? Are you a doctor? Can you guarantee Brian's knee won't get worse?"

She wanted to tell him there was no reason to doubt that corrective surgery would restore Brian's knee, but that was none of Ralph's business. She'd come here determined to keep Brian out of the conversation as much as possible. "Did your so-called source hint that Brian would become a cripple?" she challenged. "Or did you make that up on your own?"

"Are you saying I made up that article? That's a serious charge, young lady."

"And you made a serious mistake writing what you did." Dawn clenched her fists, surprised at and yet understanding the extent of her anger.

Instead of him answering, Ralph's eyes strayed to the outer room. His mouth twitched and his eyes narrowed. "It looks as if the rest of our little party has arrived."

Dawn turned. She felt her heart leap as Brian made his way toward Ralph's cubicle. What was he doing here? she wondered.

Brian opened the door and entered without waiting for an invitation. For several moments his eyes locked with Dawn's, giving no quarter. "You're here," he said flatly. "But then I guess I shouldn't be surprised, should I?"

Dawn opened her mouth to speak, but Brian cut her off. "I'm in a hurry," he snapped. "You and Ralph will have to continue your conversation when I'm done. After all," he said, turning toward the reporter, "I did have an appointment."

Ralph glanced at his watch. Dawn thought she noted a slight twitching of his lips as he did. "I'm running against a deadline," Ralph said. "I suggest you keep this short."

"I won't be here longer than I have to." Brian pulled an envelope out of his pocket and waved it under Ralph's nose. "I want you to read this. Then I want a retraction."

"What is it?" Ralph pulled away slightly.

"It's a letter from the surgeon you referred to in your so-called article. It says, in brief, that one Dr. Halston examined me this morning. After taking X rays he's convinced that my condition is completely reversible. If you don't make this public, I'm going to take it to the editor. He is your boss, isn't he?"

Silence spread over the small room. Dimly Dawn heard the sounds of activity from outside the glass enclosure, but she was unable to take her eyes off Brian. Ever since he'd walked into the room her senses had been alerted. Despite herself she was responding to the hard set of his shoulders, the determined look in his eyes. No longer was he a crazy man raging at her because he felt she was responsible for threatening his future with his son. He'd taken control of the situation and was going about remedying the harm Ralph's article had done. She stared at his mouth, remembering despite herself how those lips felt when they were soft and not caught in an angry line.

"Did Dr. Halston really say that?" she pressed. "You are going to be all right?"

Brian glanced at her but didn't answer. Instead, he leaned forward on Ralph's desk until the men's faces were only inches apart. "Have I made myself clear?" he pressed. "I know the paper's editorial policy. Your boss isn't about to condone that brand of irresponsible journalism. I demand a retraction."

"My source—" Ralph stammered.

"Your so-called source be damned!" Brian shot back, his eyes flickering briefly on Dawn. "Either your source lied, or you took conjecture and blew it out of proportion. Twisted it to meet your need. Well? I'm waiting. What is it going to be? Will the retraction be in tonight's paper, or do I have to make that appointment with your boss?"

Ralph's eyes pulled away from Brian's and settled on Dawn. "I didn't mean any harm," Ralph offered weakly.

"The hell you didn't! You told the whole county that I was headed for a wheelchair. Why did you think that would do anything but damage what I've been working to build?"

"My source assured me—"

Again Brian stopped him. "I don't want to hear that word again!" he said as Dawn stiffened her back against the impact of those words. "Your source was either stupid or incredibly naive to come to you with a piece of information you might twist to your advantage. I don't know if you know it or not, but I'm going to court tomorrow to ask for custody of my son. One way or another you're going to undo the damage you've done!"

"It might be too late. Maybe tomorrow—"

"Tomorrow could be too late for me," Brian pointed out, putting the force of his physique behind his words. "The retraction will be in today's paper. Understand?" He paused to let his words sink in and then continued. "I have a great deal to do today. I'm leaving now so you can write that article."

He turned toward Dawn. "I suggest you do the

same thing, Miss Morrell," he said, the words lashing around Dawn like a whip. "I don't believe you have any further usefulness as far as the sports department is concerned."

Dawn started to rise from her chair, but Brian held her down. "I don't know what you're doing here. I would have thought you and Ralph had already conducted whatever business you had."

"Jump to any conclusion you want," Dawn said, determined not to let him know she wasn't immune to the impact of his touch. "It's a peculiar knack of yours."

"Will you get off her back!" Ralph snapped. "I don't know what's going on between you two, but leave me out of it. Anything you two have to work out can be done on your own time, and someplace else."

Brian released Dawn. "You're right," Brian said as he reached for the door. "Dawn and I have some things to work out. But not today. I have a court date that comes first."

He had opened the door and was moving through it when Dawn surged to her feet and stopped him with viselike fingers. She waited until he'd turned and was facing her.

"Fight for your son, Brian. He's worth everything."

A cloud passed over Brian's face and for a moment she thought she saw something she almost understood flickering in his eyes. He didn't pull away but simply stared down at her. "You're right," he said softly. "Tad is everything to me. At least he has been since he was born. Sometimes that blinds me to other things."

When he turned away this time, Dawn didn't try to stop him. Instead, she let her whisper follow him out the door. "Fight for your son."

"I've seen sparks in my life, but this beats them all," Ralph was saying from somewhere behind her. With an effort Dawn pulled her eyes away from Brian's departing back and concentrated on what Ralph was saying.

"He loves his son," she said, her heart forming the words. "Tad is his life."

"I'm not so sure of that," Ralph replied. "Maybe that was true a few months ago, but it looks like someone else is keeping him up nights these days."

Was Ralph talking about her? No! she told herself. What fragile start they'd had in a motel had died a quick and painful death. Brian believed her guilty of betrayal. "Why did you do it?" she had to ask Ralph. Maybe the truth was coming too late to change anything, but for the sake of her sanity she had to know.

"It was a story. A hell of a story." Ralph shrugged, his face aging in the process. "Looks like I'll have to print a retraction. That happens sometimes."

"I still don't understand why you did it," Dawn repeated, finding it difficult to speak because something of Brian remained in the room.

. "You aren't in this business." Ralph was leaning back in his chair again. "You haven't had to face one deadline after another, an editor who wants more than the scores of the local Babe Ruth teams. I was given a juicy little tidbit to bite on. Can you blame me for making it more than it was?" His smile was a bitter one, which only accented the lines of his face. "I'll write the damn retraction all right. But I'm not going to bury myself in the process. The article's going to say that I did further research and this is what I learned. Your friend isn't going to care as long as he comes out of it healthy. And I keep my job.''

Dawn stared at the reporter. He was more complex than she'd imagined. Ralph was an aging man fighting to stay up with the competition. She now realized that his blatant attempt to seduce her was nothing more than a need to prove his masculinity to himself.

"Do you mind if I ask you something?" she asked, and then waved her hand at him. "I don't care if you mind. I'm going to ask it anyway. Brian thought I was your source. Who was? How did you learn about Brian's knee?"

Ralph's laugh was bitter. "That little tidbit, my dear, was dropped straight into my lap. I didn't have to do a damn bit of work to get it. Think. I believe you can figure it out yourself."

Dawn stared, concentrating. There was only one person, to her knowledge, who might have a reason to harm Brian. "Big Bob?"

"Bingo! He walked in here big as life the other day. Dropped the whole thing on me."

"But how did he find out?" Dawn's need to have the mystery explained took precedence, momentarily, over the pain she was feeling inside. "I'm the only one who knew about Brian's knee. He—I'm sure he didn't tell anyone else."

"That's where you're wrong." Ralph nodded. "Maybe Riegel didn't come out and roll up his pant leg around someone else, but there's no way he could have kept his condition from those around him. Big Bob saw him limping a couple of times. He started putting things together. He had a reason when Brian gave him the ax.''

"I still don't understand. You knew the name of the doctor Brian was going to. It made the article sound factual."

"You really aren't going to give up until you've put all the pieces together, are you? Okay. Here's the final chapter as I understand it. Brian called Big Bob into his office to lay the bad news on him. There was a piece of paper on the desk with the name of a doctor on it. Later Bob called around and learned that Dr. Halston specialized in reconstructive surgery. Bingo!"

Dawn had put that note on Brian's desk. She'd provided the final link. Unknowingly she'd given Bob what he was looking for, and it very nearly destroyed Brian's chances for his son in the process.

Thank God Brian was fighting back!

Slowly, unthinking, Dawn picked up her purse and stumbled out the door. Ralph called after her, but she didn't respond. She felt relief because she was fairly certain Ralph would write the article needed to give Brian a fighting chance in court tomorrow. But that still didn't stop her from remembering the look on his face when he walked into Ralph's office and saw her there. His eyes said that she was the last person in the world he wanted to be in the same room with.

Why? Did he hate her that much? she wondered.

Dawn honestly didn't remember driving home. She came out of her lethargy only as she was unlocking the door and walking into her empty house. If only her mother wasn't on her honeymoon! She needed, desperately, to have someone to talk to. Not that she could have told her mother what she was feeling inside. Those feelings had to be kept locked up or they would shatter her. But another voice, a loving mother saying something to make her laugh, would go a long way toward helping her get through the day.

But Crystal was on her honeymoon, and Dawn had an empty day—an empty life—stretching ahead of her.

Well, what did she expect? Only a fool would allow her entire being to become committed to a man who first ignored her and then offered her only one day at a time. He'd tried to warn her, hadn't he? Looking back she now believed she could see the silent warnings. He'd been friendly enough the first night, when they'd shared a pizza together, two old friends meeting after a separation of years. But after that he'd drawn back, become remote, cruel even. The night in the motel had been only one night, a time to dream, to spin hopes out of silken threads. But like Cinderella, the striking of the clock signaled a return to the world of reality.

Real men and women don't hitch their star to one romantic night. For Brian it had been a simple diversion, a way to forget the responsibilities of work, his concerns for his son. He'd come to her because she offered—oh, how willingly—a magic night without responsibility.

It was a magic night! At least she had that memory. But it had nothing to do with what faced them in the morning.

Fool! She'd thought she'd said good-bye to the starry-eyed teenager who fell in love with a man she'd made out of her dreams. But she'd been wrong. The romantic teenager was still around, still hiding her eyes and her heart from reality.

Brian was concerned with his job and his son. What made her think he would carry her away on a white charger to live untouched by reality?

It was too much to think about! Desperate because she knew there were only tears waiting in the house, Dawn changed quickly and threw on a sleeveless top and high-cut shorts. Running had been her salvation before. It had to work today. It had to!

She ran with a vengeance, trying to force away the heartbreaking thoughts that threatened to engulf her. Her feet pounded furiously on the pavement as she made her way out of the city limits and into the rolling hills covered with pear orchards. The air was warm to her lungs and flesh, but she didn't let that stop her. She wanted to run until she dropped.

After the first two miles, she was no longer being haunted by her final memory of Brian. She forced herself to concentrate on the landscape passing slowly on both sides. Some of the orchards, she knew, had been in production for over a hundred years. It gave a sense of permanence to a world she feared was slipping away from her. This late in the spring the trees had already shed their blossoms. The fruit that would soon grace the tables of both local residents and the recipients of gift baskets, sent hundreds, even thousands of miles, was hidden by the rich green foliage.

The name Verdue sprang to Dawn's mind, but she shook it off. As she jogged along the seldom-used country road she glanced down the long rows of fruit trees, looking for the migrant workers who might be thinning, watering, or spraying the trees. The smiling dark-skinned Mexicans made her feel uneasy as a child, mostly because she didn't understand their language. But now she envied their acceptance of their place in life's scheme. Most of them worked hard to send money back to their families in Mexico. And if they brought their wives and children with them, they sent their children off to school to learn English. Even now she could see a trio of preschool boys playing under the shelter of the laden trees. Working nearby were men who could lift a child in their arms as easily as they did the tools they carried with them.

It seemed inconceivable that there'd been a time when men weren't considered real men if they took an active role in raising their children. Dawn never failed to respond when she saw a man with his children by his side, a baby in his arms. It was right—the ultimate reward for becoming a man.

Dawn tossed her head skyward as her eyes followed the flight of a pheasant startled from its resting place in the high grass. She tried to concentrate on the sense of freedom the colorful male exuded, but there was no shaking off the other thought. If Ralph wrote what he had to, if the hearing in the judge's chambers came out the way Brian wanted, he would soon have his son to raise and not just for fleeting, precious visits.

Fight for your son, she'd told him. Dawn knew Brian well enough that she didn't doubt that he'd go before the judge prepared to prove himself as a worthy parent. Dawn knew almost nothing about Tad's mother, but she believed Brian would have stepped aside if he felt his ex-wife was fit to raise their child.

But that wasn't what he was doing. And because Brian felt the need to become responsible for Tad, Dawn was convinced it was in Tad's best interest.

Fight for your son. Become a family, she thought.

Dawn ran over two hours that day. When she finally returned home, the turmoil she'd taken with her had been replaced by a strange calm. Tension had left her, leaving her in an accepting mood. She loved Brian; she would probably always love him.

But wanting love and having it didn't always happen.

Chapter Twelve

When the newspaper came out, Dawn bought a copy and opened to the sports section. The article with the headline FUTURE BRIGHTENS FOR GENERAL MANAGER was everything Ralph said it would be. Dawn had to laugh because Ralph had carefully worded the article to make it sound as if he'd dug through a web of secrecy until he'd uncovered the truth. "Surgery probably is in Riegel's future," the article said. "But the grim prognosis of two days ago has changed to one of optimism." The article went on to describe how scar tissue from Brian's previous surgery was causing his problems but could be remedied. The medical information came right from the letter Brian had dropped on Ralph's desk, but Ralph didn't mention that.

It didn't matter. Now it was public knowledge that the manager of the Northwest A's wasn't in danger of becoming a cripple after all. The article made no mention of Brian asking for custody of his son, for which Dawn was grateful and a little surprised, given Ralph's love of gossip. That should remain a private matter between a judge and the parties involved.

Since no game was scheduled for the evening,

Dawn spent it at home, puttering around in her fenced backyard, her ear alerted for the phone. Did she really expect Brian to call her? Although logic answered no, her heart refused to accept the answer. She wanted to call Brian and tell him of the hand Big Bob had had in the mess with Ralph, but she held back. Brian would be going to court in the morning. That was enough for him to concentrate on, not having to listen to a woman tell him that he'd jumped at the wrong conclusion.

What he felt for her wasn't strong enough to stand in the face of circumstantial evidence. If he loved her as she loved him, he'd have known she could never be a party, even remotely, to the lies Ralph had written.

That was the reality that kept Dawn's hands off the telephone. Love trusts. It doesn't bend and twist, no matter how much it is tested. She realized that Brian would react adversely to something that could cost him his son. What parent wouldn't? But he'd suspected her. It hurt! More than she dared to admit, even to herself.

Brian hadn't been ready to trust her and because of that, the fragile bud of their revitalized love would never bloom into adulthood.

The painful truth tore at Dawn, leaving her feeling as if she'd been subjected to a physical beating, but because it was the truth, she realized she had no choice but to accept what wouldn't be changed.

She'd continue to work with the team until the end of the season, not because it was written into her contract, but because Dawn Morrell wasn't a quitter. During that time she'd keep her heart wrapped in a thick protective blanket, taking care not to look into Brian's eyes. She'd force herself not to think about lying in his arms, being swept away into a world of endless sunrises. Somehow—somehow she wouldn't allow herself to fall asleep with her flesh recording his touch, his gentle and yet total assault on her senses.

If only it wasn't so hard! she thought.

The next day was a hot one, which meant Dawn would have to be alert to the possibility of sunstroke, heat exhaustion, and even cramps brought on by loss of body salt. She reviewed her first aid literature on treating those conditions and called ahead to make sure she would be supplied with ice when deliveries were made to the concession stand. But even as she worked, her eyes continued to stray to the clock. When would Brian be going before the judge? She felt some of the tension she was sure Brian was experiencing. If only there was something she could do to help. If only she could tell him she realized what he was going through. She hadn't been embroiled in a custody suit, but she'd gone through the agony of not knowing whether Jim would live. Deep down those raw emotions were the same.

She wished she knew more about court matters where children were involved. Naturally a child custody case wouldn't make the news. How and when would she know of the outcome? A week ago she would have heard directly from Brian, but his silence was all the message she needed. He wanted nothing to do with her. She wasn't part of his life.

She arrived at Verdue Field early, chafing because she had had little to do until the players began to arrive. Maybe Coach Weatherby would know if the hearing was over, she kept thinking. She hated having to admit to the sweet man that the budding romance he'd been in favor of was no more, but her pride wasn't the important thing. Finding out whether Brian would become a full-time father was.

"I'm surprised to see you here," Coach Weatherby said as he greeted her.

"You are? The temperature is a factor tonight. I want to be nearby in case someone gets too much heat."

"Keep a close eye on the catcher. He's the one who really suffers. Of course, there might be some people in the stands who aren't prepared for the temperature change. No, I thought you might have taken off with Brian."

Brian took off! What did that mean? Dawn wanted to know. "He—he isn't going to be here tonight?" she stammered, her heart pounding.

"He didn't tell you? Ah, child, what happened between the two of you? Don't tell me." The manager wrapped a protective arm around Dawn's shoulders. "It's in your eyes. Things aren't working out for you two, are they?"

Numbly she shook her head. "Where is he?" she whispered.

"He called about an hour ago. He's headed for the coast to do some camping. He'll be back in a week, he said."

He lost! Brian didn't get his son! "How did he sound?"

"Like a kid at Christmas." The manager grinned. "For a grown man with a world of responsibility on his shoulders, he sounded an awful lot like someone who just broke into a candy store."

Dawn stifled an urge to throttle Coach Weatherby. He was rambling on, not telling her what she had to hear. "Is he going alone?"

"Of course not. Why do you think he's walking ten feet off the ground? Tad's with him." He sobered. "I kind of thought the three of you might be off getting to know each other better."

Dawn blushed slightly at the manager's easy assumption that an unmarried man and woman would go off camping together, but the thought was only a fleeting one. "What did he tell you?" she asked, feeling like a drowning woman grasping at straws.

"About the custody thing? Not much. He said he was throwing things together as fast as he could. He was in one hell of a hurry to get the boy where he could have him to himself. He did tell me that the hearing took about a half hour. Something about his ex-wife showing up late and then yelling because she'd be damned if she'd let Brian win. Made a poor showing of herself, I take it."

"It isn't a contest," Dawn managed, despite her whirling emotions. "Tad's future is the only thing that matters."

"That's what Brian said. I guess he told the judge he wanted Tad to grow up in a loving home. At least that's what I got out of the conversation. That's why he wanted custody, not because he wanted to punish the boy's mother." Coach Weatherby nodded vigorously. "I guess Brian made his point all right. Anyway, he's taking Tad with him so they can get away from things for a few days. He said the boy's confused and needs to talk about what's been happening."

Say it, Dawn moaned silently. *Brian wants to get away from me too.* Then because she knew her life would be agony unless she knew, she asked the question. "Did he say anything about me?"

"I'm sorry, honey. No. I figured it was because you were going with him. Hey, look, kid." He offered Dawn the comfort of his bony chest. "He'll be back in a week. You can talk then. He's just got a lot on his mind now, what with helping Tad get his life in order and everything. He has to put the boy first."

"I know that," Dawn managed from the shelter of the manager's chest. But the words gave her little comfort. If Brian found time to call Coach Weatherby, he had time to get in touch with her.

But he hadn't. He'd left still believing she was responsible for that horrible newspaper article. Dawn accepted her own small, unwilling role in it. She probably shouldn't have left the doctor's name and number where others could see it. But Brian had to know she loved him too much to ever do anything that might cause him harm. He had to! she thought.

For the next three days Dawn moved through a cruel limbo, functioning on a professional level, iron will forcing her not to think of a man and his son on a camping trip. She looked after her mother's house, worked in her own yard, even accepted an invitation from a local health club to talk on sports medicine. But through it all she felt as if she'd placed her heart in a windowless cage that might suddenly disintegrate, leaving her exposed and shattered.

The players were unusually kind to her, and she

wondered if the manager had said something. They seemed to go out of their way to include her in their free-time activities and insisted she join them for a pizza. "You aren't a ballplayer unless you eat pizza," she was informed. "Hell, they won't even let you into Verdue Field unless you have cheese sticking to your chin."

She went along with the challenge, but it was a particularly unnerving experience because, unknowing, she was certain, the players chose the same pizza parlor Brian had taken her to that first night.

But hard as the evening was, the night that followed was worse. If only her body didn't remember so completely the ecstasy of what it felt like to be in Brian's arms. There was no fighting the memory of his strong legs naked on her bed as she treated his injured knee. She could still feel his fingers laced through her hair, his lips seeking hers. His hands were on her trembling flesh, bearing messages—messages she'd interpreted as love.

How wrong she'd been! One day at a time. Why hadn't her heart listened?

Dawn was both grateful and apprehensive when her mother called to say they were returning from their honeymoon and would Dawn please join them for a quiet dinner. She tried to plead work as an excuse, but Crystal only said they'd eat early enough that Dawn wouldn't be delayed in getting to Verdue Field. "Don't you want us to bore you to death with our pictures?" Crystal asked. "Besides, we picked you up a little something. I'll pout and carry on if you don't tell me what wonderful taste in gifts I have."

The gift turned out to be a picture of one of the

current greats of baseball, personally autographed. "We went to a pro game," Crystal explained. "See what you've done to me? You've turned me into a baseball nut. I told the player I wanted the autograph for my little girl. He stared at my gray hairs, but he did it anyway. He even wrote something on the back for you."

Dawn turned it over. "Forget the sacrifice bunt. Go for the grand slam."

"He probably writes that all the time," Peter supplied. "But it makes sense, don't you think? It has to do with reaching for all you can get out of life. Your mom told me you worked yourself out of traditional medicine, got a job you really enjoy. That sounds like a line drive double at least to me."

Dawn's smile was forced. She felt a sudden chill because the written words paralleled her recent thoughts. How could the ballplayer have known? The future she'd been forced to face for the past three days more closely resembled a sacrifice bunt than a home run. "It's interesting advice," she managed shakily. "It's a shame most of us never hit that grand slam."

Crystal gave her daughter a puzzled, concerned look but asked no questions. Somehow Dawn made it through the meal, but her mother and new stepfather would never know the effort it cost.

They were so deeply in love, so happy simply to be around each other. When they touched, something magic passed between their eyes. Dawn didn't even ask herself whether she was capable of feeling that magic. She knew the answer. Her heart had only loved one man.

But that man was unattainable. Whatever the rest

of her life held, it would never be that perfect grand slam.

Fortunately, the evening's game cut short Dawn's need to maintain some semblance of cheer for her mother's sake. She complimented the meal, exclaimed over pictures of sunsets, forests, and slightly out of focus motels, and asked enough questions to show she really was interested in their trip. Thinking about the glow on her mother's face made it easier to get through an evening without Brian at Verdue Field.

She was still asleep the next morning when the phone rang. It was the man from the local radio station who provided game coverage. Apparently, he and Brian had been working on plans to improve the communications system from Verdue Field to the station. The new system hadn't been expected for another week, but it was here and ready to be delivered to the field. The sportscaster hadn't been able to locate the grounds keeper. Did Dawn have access to the field, and could she meet him there in an hour?

Dawn groaned and crawled out of bed. She was relieved that they'd called her instead of Coach Weatherby, but it meant hurrying through a shower and facing commuter traffic. She yanked a white knit top over her head and slipped into a faded pair of jeans. What did it matter that her hair was charged with electricity? She was only going to be around long enough to open a few doors.

The trip wound up taking three hours. When she saw the men from the electric company trying to drive their truck into Verdue Field to complete the necessary connections, she was afraid they'd drive out onto the playing field unless she stayed around to make sure that kind of carelessness didn't take place. She was interested in the advanced communication equipment but nervous because she was responsible for the actions of the men swarming around the press box. Although she tried to stay out of the way, it seemed as if someone was always asking her advice about one thing or another. "I'm not the general manager," she repeated more than once, but no one seemed to be listening.

When the last man was leaving, Dawn sank into one of the box seats and stared glassy-eyed at the field below her. After all the noise and confusion, the silence was a welcome contrast. Her head still throbbed from having to stand so close to power tools, and the hollow feeling she felt in her stomach reminded her that she hadn't had breakfast. But then except for pizza and the dinner with her mother, she hadn't had much to eat since Brian left.

The truth was, she hadn't felt alive enough to concentrate on something as mundane as food in the past few days. Dawn blinked slowly, trying to concentrate. The charm of Verdue Field still existed, but something—some magic quality—was gone. The grass was still as green, the distant outfield fences still as imposing. The fresh paint on the seats gave them a crisp new look. The problem was that Dawn felt neither crisp nor new. She was drained, sinking in a lethargy she had scant control over.

And all because her heart wouldn't let go of Brian.

Tears forced themselves up from their hiding place deep inside and for once Dawn didn't try to fight them. Instead, she dropped her head and buried her face in her strangely cold hands. It shouldn't hurt like this! She was a grown woman. She should have better control over her emotions, her heart.

But she didn't. The love she felt for Brian was something that had simmered unknown for ten years. Reawakening it had been her undoing and now she had to pay the price.

A sound, slight but unmistakable, reached her. Dawn lifted her wet face and wiped away what she could of her tears. Because her vision was blurry, it took a few minutes before she realized it was a small boy she saw down on the field. She stood up, feeling responsible because she had been the one to leave the entrance open. She was about to inform him that unfortunately Verdue Field wasn't a child's playground when she realized who the boy was. Tad!

If Tad was here, it meant his father was too.

Maybe she could slip away without him seeing her. But her car was out front. He had to have seen that. There was no way she could escape.

And did she want to, really? The hours without him had been a brand of agony unlike any she'd experienced since she was a girl and realized Brian wasn't going to call and ask to see her again. It no longer mattered that their time together had ended all too soon. She needed to see him again in order to record the final out in that inning of her life.

Maybe then she could accept what she knew she'd see in his eyes. He didn't love her. Her heart would see, would start to accept.

Before she could move she saw him come around a corner and start up the stairs toward her. Her breath caught in her throat at the sight. Nothing about him had changed, and yet seeing him did things to her senses she had pitifully little control over. She didn't even try to speak as he neared her.

She could tell he was favoring his knee, but because she knew his discomfort would soon end, it no longer tore her apart to see the effort it took for him to walk. His shirt was open at the throat to accommodate the heat, but all Dawn was aware of were the fine hairs she'd once been able to touch. Gone from his face were the lines of responsibility and concern. He had his son. His joy in that fact was plain. What he might feel for her was safely hidden.

"I went to your place this morning," he said when he was near enough for her to hear. "What are you doing here?"

She knew she should be telling him about the revamped radio equipment, but somehow it didn't seem worth the effort. "Why were you there?" Didn't he know how hard it was for her to talk?

"There's something I want to say to you." Instead of continuing, he sat in the box seat next to her and leaned forward so he could watch his son. Their shoulders touched. It took all Dawn's will not to reach out and caress that precious shoulder. She ached with desire, a desire she must keep from him. That night in a motel had made her a woman, and that woman knew all too well that only the intertwining of their bodies would satisfy her longing. But that wasn't to be.

Brian was silent too for over a minute, but there was no way she could know what he was thinking. Then he said, "Remember how you ran the bases that first day? Tad loves doing that."

Dawn nodded. The boy below them was sliding into

second in a perfect imitation of what professional ball-players did. "Maybe he'll play one day," she said because she felt something was expected of her. If he touched her, even looked at her, she was afraid she'd fall apart. Outwardly she retained some semblance of composure. Inside it was another story.

"Do you want to hear about our camping trip?"

I want to hear what you're thinking. I want to know if my living still has a purpose. Instead, she said, "My mother was on her honeymoon. I saw her pictures, but she didn't go camping."

Brian shook his head, still watching his son. "I didn't take any pictures." He laughed. "Tad didn't sit still long enough for that. I was going to stay a week."

"Why didn't you?"

"There's something I haven't settled yet." At last he turned to her. "It has to do with you."

Was he thinking about their last meeting in Ralph's office, when his eyes had ripped her into shreds? She could tell him of Big Bob's role in what happened, but she didn't. It no longer mattered. If Brian didn't love her, the truth wouldn't change anything. "What did you and Tad do while you were gone?" she asked, desperately grasping for a safe topic. She wasn't ready to hear what she knew would end things. Stalling put off the inevitable.

Brian told her about pitching a tent and camping near the ocean. They'd rented a fishing boat and gone out, just the two of them. Because the ocean was calm that day, they stayed out for hours, feeding sea gulls, looking for whales so Tad would have something to tell his friends, even hooking a fish and letting Tad reel it in "all by himself."

Throughout the narrative Dawn concentrated more on the emotion in Brian's voice than his actual words. His joy at being able to share those days with his son was obvious. Although he tried to maintain an air of dignity, it was clear that the experience was all he hoped it would be. "I love being a father," he finished up. "There's nothing else that gives me greater satisfaction. I'm seeing the world through his eyes. It's my second childhood."

It's the grand slam in your life, Dawn thought, fighting tears. She remembered what it felt like to have Tad's little arms wrapped around her neck and understood what Brian was experiencing. The only thing she didn't know was what it was like to be that child's mother. "I'm happy for you," she managed. "It sounds like you had a wonderful time."

"We did. Dawn, something happened while I was cut off from the world." His eyes locked with hers and wouldn't let go. "I finally admitted something about myself. And about you."

She trembled under his gaze, her whole being suspended in time. Brian held her heart in his hands.

"Do you remember when we were in Ralph's office?"

She locked her hands tightly together in her lap. It was coming. Any minute now she'd hear that their night had been a mistake—a fairy tale and not reality. "How can I forget. You hated me."

Instead of agreeing, he shook his head as if he were trying to collect his senses. "I don't know what I was thinking that day. I was so damn worked up, I can't remember half of what I was saying. I couldn't be sure Ralph would listen to reason and so much hinged on an article that told the truth. Hell, I kept telling myself I had the doctor's report going for me, that Ralph couldn't deny that. But when I saw you in there with him—it got me going all over again. I said, did, some things I shouldn't have."

"You didn't let me say much." She didn't want to sound as if she were accusing him, but her emotions were too raw to control.

"I sure as hell didn't. You were trying to tell me something, only I wouldn't listen. But at least I got my point across with Ralph. The second article helped. The judge told me it figured in his decision. When I heard him say Tad could live with me, all I wanted to do was grab my boy and get away from everything."

"From me. You wanted to get away from me." It wasn't a question.

Brian frowned. "Things were happening so damn fast. I stood still long enough to realize how wrong I'd been to accuse you. I remembered what you said about fighting for Tad. You didn't have to. You wouldn't have if you hadn't meant it. I realized how much it must have cost you to speak after the way I treated you." He paused. "I started putting the pieces together. Before Tad and I took off I called Ralph. He confirmed my suspicions about why you were there. Ralph said you were raking him over the coals when I showed up."

"You knew I didn't have anything to do with the article? But you still left without talking to me." She should get up, walk away. But her legs lacked the strength. It was as if Brian were possessed of a magnetic force that held her, quivering, just outside the circle of his arms.

Brian sighed. "Do you remember what I said about one day at a time? A long time ago I convinced myself that was how I should run my life. No longtime commitments. I committed myself to a woman once and it didn't work out. Hell! Marrying her was the biggest mistake of my life. Tad's the only good thing that came out of it. I'm committed to my son and my job, but I kept telling myself I wasn't ever going to get close to a woman again. That's when I came up with the brilliant deduction that I could take life twenty-four hours a day as far as you were concerned and it would work out."

"A sacrifice bunt," Dawn said without thinking.

"What?"

"It's some advice I was given yesterday. Don't settle for the sacrifice bunt. Go for the grand slam." Dawn blinked back tears.

Maybe today, this moment, was her only chance. Brian had said nothing about his feelings for her, why he felt the need to get away from her. But if she didn't find out, she'd spend the rest of her life feeling as if she'd never taken the swing that could be either a strikeout or much, much more.

Summoning all the strength left in her ravaged senses, Dawn reached out and lightly touched Brian's shoulder. Her reaction to the contact was instantaneous. His effect on her hadn't changed. She wanted him, needed his embrace to feel alive. She had to close her eyes in order to be able to speak. "Why did you want to get away from me?"

"I didn't trust my reactions to you. I needed time to think."

"What did you learn?"

Suddenly Dawn was in Brian's arms. Her eyes flew open, but all she could see was the outline of his chest. Knowing how naked her desire must be to him, she nonetheless gave in to the sweet ecstasy of his strength. Her breathing was something she had scant control over. Only by drawing deeply through her nostrils could she hope to keep from surrendering her body to this man. She tilted her head up, and their lips met.

Dawn was caught in the spell cast by Brian's presence. His lips were restoring her to life, spiriting her to a peak of happiness she thought she'd lost forever. Her arms found their way around his neck, pulling him close so he could feel her need. It was dangerous for her to be presenting her desire, but she was beyond caring. She felt his hands on her back, holding her tight against him, and sobbed because she'd never wanted anything as much as she wanted what was happening this moment. The pounding of her blood in her temples, beating out a tattoo, made her dizzy. She could almost believe that she had no need to exist beyond the present.

But he still hadn't given her an answer. And Dawn needed more than a kiss to hinge the rest of her life on. She pushed herself away, breaking the contact of their lips, and gazed up into his eyes. The incredible, perfect answer was there.

"I love you," he whispered as they came together again.

"You—you mean it?"

"Why are you asking?" He held her in strong arms, not allowing her to think of anything except him. His eyes were on her full lips, her breasts, telegraphing his own emotions. "Oh, God, you don't love me!"

"I love you! I've always loved you!" She bared her deepest secret, but it didn't matter. She was swinging for that once in a lifetime grand slam.

"And I've always loved you." He crushed her against his chest, his arms enveloping her. Despite the fabric separating their flesh, she could feel his body heat and reacted to it. "Ten years ago I fell in love with a white angel. Nothing has changed that." He took a deep breath. "That's what I finally admitted while I was away from you, when I could think without you around me. Until then I'd tried to tell myself that love can't continue for ten years, not if the people are separated by hundreds of miles. I married someone else, someone I thought I loved. When I saw you again, I refused to acknowledge the way I felt. I wouldn't let myself listen to what my heart was trying to tell me. That's why I tried to hold you at arm's length."

Brian groaned. "God, what a fool I was. One day at a time? That's like wanting to be half alive, not mapping out any kind of future. I don't want to live my life that way."

"Neither do I." She could hear the solid crack of bat against ball. "Don't let me go. Please, don't ever let me go!"

"I won't, my white angel. I'm not ever going to risk losing you again." His fingers traced the outline of her jaw, brushed down her neck, and found the silken swell of her breast. Dawn felt no desire to make him stop. Her body had grown from a child's to that of a woman. The woman in her knew how right his touch was. "I love you," she whispered, her voice blending with the beating of her heart.

Their embrace might have become much more if they hadn't been aware of the small figure coming up the stairs to join them in the stands above Verdue Field. Dawn opened her eyes and gazed down at the mirror image of the man she loved. Her hand went out and enveloped Tad's small one. "What do you want, son?" she heard Brian say.

"Are you going to kiss all day? I'm hungry."

Dawn threw back her head and laughed. The ball was sailing toward the center field fence, its arc high and proud and strong. "What did you have in mind?"

"Ice cream!"

"Ice cream it is." Brian laughed as he swung his son onto his hip. His free hand found Dawn's. "And after we eat, we're going to talk about all of us becoming a family."

As they reached the bottom of the stairs Dawn looked out at Verdue Field. She could see the crowd rising to its feet as the home run ball cleared the distant fence.

She had her grand slam.